Grandma's stories, '…would always start in the place where we were,' and so it is with *Unusual Places*. Human remains are concealed in the Greenwich Tunnel in a world where London is a prison; a market is the setting for sexual and sensual awakenings; a professional picnicker finds love. Louise Tondeur's stories skip along, rich with detail and musical prose, only to trip us up with turns and surprises: the unusual lurks in the most ordinary of places.

❦

Louise Tondeur has been a writer and a teacher in various guises for the last twenty-five years. She lives in East Sussex and is currently working on her first crime novel.

These are the stories you might feel surging around you as you walk down a crowded city street, every one its own world of tenderness, violence, absurdity and joy.

Joanne Limburg, author of *Small Pieces, A Want of Kindness* and *The Woman Who Thought Too Much*

Tondeur's eye for detail is so precise, you might fear being in her presence, lest she see your secrets, too. What a tender, dark, nuanced book: a quiet storm.

Leone Ross, author of *Come Let Us Sing Anyway, All the Blood is Red* and *Orange Laughter*

❦

About *The Haven Home for Delinquent Girls:*

Tondeur's brand of homespun gothic and seaside camp is a memorable one … tender and eccentric.

The Independent

She manages an intriguing blend of nostalgia and knowingness, reminiscent of Todd Haynes's film, Far From Heaven.

Times Literary Supplement

Also by Louise Tondeur

The Haven Home for Delinquent Girls (Review, 2004)
The Water's Edge (Review, 2003)

To Sarah and Zachary

Unusual Places

Louise Tondeur

Louise Tondeur

Cultured Llama Publishing

First published in 2018 by
Cultured Llama Publishing
www.culturedllama.co.uk

A CIP record for this book is available from The British Library

ISBN 978-0-9957381-9-5

Printed in Great Britain by Lightning Source UK Ltd

Cover design: Mark Holihan

Photography: Ana Bohane Photography (www.anabohane.com)

Contents

Part One

A Professional Picnicker Meets Her True Love

I am a professional picnicker. I picnic freelance, and write for magazines about it. Pretty soon after I started, marketing departments and PR companies got interested, and now I try out their products for a fee, kitchen equipment, food storage products, luxury picnic items, that kind of thing. It isn't just a job, I prefer it anyway: to take my food outside to where the flowers are deep blue baby pompoms and pink and white triffids, or where sluttish tulips shake their heads like dogs with long ears next to ink-drop centred pansies. I go all over London, spreading out my cloth in Camden, Islington, Wandsworth, St. Paul's, Vauxhall, Highbury. Sometimes I'm near a river or a lake or a church, sometimes a park with a pond. I shared my biscuits with a peacock once. I like places with picnic tables, I slide my legs over the rough wood and set my food out in front of me.

Smarties in a pot, a banana, some nice crisps from Waitrose, the ones with the elaborate names, organic sea salt and cracked pepper, lemon and haddock, that kind of thing, sandwiches with their crusts cut off, maple syrup and apricot, or goats' cheese, walnut and spinach, peanut butter and strawberry jam, avocado and figs, and biscuits. I have tea in a flask. When I drink I can see my reflection in the bottom of the metal cup.

I had a picnic in January once. There was ice on the puddles. The pond was frozen over. I could see orange flashes underneath the surface. I hoped the goldfish were still alive and that their bodies weren't floating around lifeless down there, their souls unable to escape through the ice to fish heaven. Is there a fish heaven? Or does everyone go to the same heaven? There are no fish churches, temples, that kind of thing, I think, sipping my drink, looking at my face in the cup again. No fish vicars or confessionals, or perhaps they are there: under the lily pads, out in the middle of the ocean, how do we know for sure? But surely fish can live for years, and years have winters in them.

Fish hell would smell of chips, and there would be no water anywhere, but only constant flapping, useless opening of gills, no dead relief, only dying, open-mouthed.

When I went on my winter picnic, the ground was hard and white, the bench I sat on was cold. I wore my coat with the fur collar. I made hot chocolate instead of tea, and had sponge cake instead of a biscuit.

I had a picnic in a park by a river once, on a warm spring day. I spread out my blanket and people noticed me, nodded and smiled because they could see I was so organised – the checked cloth, flowers for the centre, bread on a foldable board to make sandwiches, a bowl for fruit, the smart silver flask, the picnic hamper with sections for the special knives, forks, spoons, even glasses, wrapped in tissue paper, plastic plates ties to the lid, a salt and pepper shaker. People who only had a plastic lunch box watched me jealously. The birds were singing to the flat leaves of the tress nearby, and a squirrel circled the trunk, round and round.

I had only just finished setting out my hamper when a blue plastic bag flew past me towards the river – the cheap kind you get in newsagents. I hate it when people drop rubbish. I am a responsible picnicker. I take my rubbish home, folded into my hamper. Some people throw cans, crisp packets, half eaten apples, all sorts – all along the river bank. I found a shoe once and half a can of beans.

I chased the plastic bag all the way down to the river bank, but it twirled off into the sky and I thought I had lost it. A giant willow stood on the bank with its fingers in the water. I got my breath back by leaning against its trunk, watching the light play in between the branches. I was thinking about how amazing it is that things grow. I had an onion. I was keeping it to make a salad roll, and it had begun to sprout, a bright green shoot. I cut it open and used half in a gravy. When I took the other half out again the shoot had continued to grow – dug up, cut off, selected, packaged, shelved, bought, bagged, stored, cut in half, refrigerated, and it was still alive.

I was thinking about the onion as I stepped through the branches again, brushing past the catkins, and there was a man sitting on the bank. He was wet. His face was pale. He looked dishevelled as if he had things to think about which didn't involve his clothes. His tie was askew, his damp shirt was undone, his trousers were hitched up so I could see his shins – black-haired and dripping – and his bare feet.

The blue bag reappeared. I ran after it. Now I was next to the pale wet man, and the blue plastic bag flew around us like a new shape of bird or a giant insect. I watched it, he watched it, as it flew high up in the air. The wind grabbed it, and it got caught in the willow tree. Behind me, and I pride myself on the fact that it was the first time it had ever happened, several dogs were eating my picnic.

I could hear laughing from the people with packed lunch-boxes, who hadn't spread their food on the grass for the local strays to munch on. Of course, with a bit of reworking, and some product placement, I knew it would make a good column – 'Picnic Disaster' – so I didn't chase them away.

It goes without saying that the man and I had sex under the branches of the willow tree. They acted like a curtain, the branches, so it wasn't exactly the same as sex outdoors. We talked first, of course, about where the plastic bag had come from, how it could have been a kingfisher, why he had swum across the river, what he had lost, why I let three dogs eat my lunch from exclusive aluminium plates that weren't even in the shops yet. We talked until the sun went down, and the other picnickers had left, until the park attendant locked the park doors, until everyone else was inside.

The man was gone in the morning. I woke up with a stiff neck and an aching lower back, and watched the ducks manoeuvring about in the water before retrieving my hamper and blanket. Needless to say, the man had left his phone number on a scrap of paper inside my hamper, a torn up leaflet for an avant-garde theatre performance somewhere or other. Of course, I phoned him. After such a promising beginning, who wouldn't? And now we live together in a four bedroom (if you count the box room) semi, well, end of terrace really, and have three kids at school. All because of a blue plastic bag.

Mrs Enid Fancy had worked in the plastics factory in Wanstead for thirteen years. She had started out on the line but now she was quality control. There were two buildings. The first smelt gluey and if you stayed inside for too long your head felt dizzy, your stomach felt sick. It was where the plastic was made, and the blue dye was added. The second building was where Enid worked. Some of the glue smell from the first building seeped in through the windows and under the door, not so you'd notice it, but when you went home you could sometimes feel a little queasy or have a headache. Enid used to get spots, just under her hair, when she worked on the line, but now she was quality control she didn't. She had become immune to it, she told herself. Funny that she could become immune to blue plastic. She wondered if you could get immunity from other things too. There was a biscuit factory on the other side of the industrial estate. What if she'd gone there instead, the day she left school? Got immunity from biscuits, like diplomatic immunity, someone from another country who can't get arrested. She was thinking it as she walked up and down the lines in building number two. This building was in sections – different section, different line, different product. They made toys for Christmas crackers, one of the last places in the UK to do it, tiny camels with a circle of plastic at the top, as if anyone would want to hang a small blue camel on a pendant, but what did she know? And pencil sharpeners. Enid always bought Luxury Crackers from Marks and Sparks so she wouldn't get the camel or the sharpener. She didn't want to think about work on Christmas Day.

Another line was plastic bags – the cheap ones that they give out in newsagents. Enid had a bag with cats on it that she got from Woolworths before it closed down. She thought about the brown, black and orange cats in a row as she inspected a box of blue plastic bags. She lifted out the first bag, it dispatched easily – 'dispatches easily' was on the marketing material. She tested the handles, rubbed it between her hands for ease of opening – that was on the marketing material too – 'easy to open'. She had to mark each box she tested out of five on a clipboard. 'Ease of opening' and 'dispatches easily' were categories, so was 'handles'. She shook the bag so it opened, ballooning out in front of her for a second. She tested the next bag, just to make sure. She gave the box a five, folded the bags and placed them carefully back inside the box. If you knew anything about bag testing, she thought, moving on to another box, randomly selected, adjusting her glasses, when you found a box with two of the bags disturbed, and neatly folded, then you knew your box had been tested by Enid Fancy from Wanstead.

In Stratford, Raz Sadangi was opening up early for the newspaper delivery. The new box of plastic bags came too. He ripped open the cardboard and hung the bags up through the holes. He was left with two piles of small hole-shaped blue plastic pieces. He examined them. When he peeled one of the blue hole-shapes off from the top of the pile, it was very thin. It stuck to his hand like a token, as if he had been marked out for something. He closed his hand around it and opened it again – the blue spot was still there.

'10 *Benson*,' a man at the counter said. Raz handed them over.

'And that,' the man said, putting down a copy of the *Sun* and a packet of chocolate biscuits. Raz still had the blue spot in the middle of his hand.

'You want a bag?' Raz said, feeling the luxury of saying it. For a week now he had been bag-less, and had had to say 'sorry no bags' a hundred times a day to customers, instead of the familiar question, to customers rolling their eyes or saying, 'Oh, for god's sake' at him. And now there it was again, and he was about to tear the first bag from the hooks under the till when he saw that two blue bags were already detached, and folded neatly, still in the cardboard box. He bent to pick one of them up. He felt the static stick the bag to his hand.

'That will be, let's see,' he said. He liked to work it out in his head then see if he was right when he typed it into the till, but as he stood up he realised the man had gone without paying. Raz went out onto the pavement but couldn't see him. He went in shaking his head and took out the book they kept for shoplifting and wrote down 10 *Benson and Hedges, Sun, Hobnobs* (chocolate, small). Then he tried to write a description of the man, but he couldn't remember anything about him - voice, hair, clothes, build, colour of skin, clean shaven or beard, young or old - nothing. He looked at the blue spot in the palm of his hand and flipped the shoplifting book shut. He opened a magazine about celebrities and leafed through it absentmindedly. The bag was still on the counter when Raymond came in for his cans of dog food.

Raz was thinking about his daughter's wedding, when she had been surrounded by blue flowers. Beautiful deep blue, not sea blue like the plastic. He had held one of the flowers in his hand all day long and felt so happy he could have turned into a flower himself, dancing, turning somersaults in the wind.

Raymond filled the bag from the counter with Happy Chappy dog food, paid, and left the shop. The bag stretched under the weight of the tins. Usually he brought one from home, but today he had forgotten. He wasn't sure why he had forgotten. Probably because he felt sad. That was it. Sad. He tossed the word around inside his head like a ping pong ball. He swung the bag as he went across the road and, distracted by a terrier that ran out in front of a car, which only just missed him, he swung it too high, and the handles of the bag broke. Cans of Happy Chappy tumbled down the road. The terrier barked loudly and ran away. Raymond gathered the cans up with the broken bag and hugged them close for rest of the way back home.

Out in the garden there was a cross. One of the care assistants had made it. Alfie had put some flowers around it. Bernadette had written one of those poems that doesn't rhyme and had pinned it to the cross. Marcel wanted to do something, so a care assistant had helped him make an origami frog out of newspaper. Raymond arranged the cans of Happy Chappy around the cross.

'There you go,' he said. 'Food for you.'

'Raymond,' one of the care assistants called. He turned around as she came over. 'He won't need his food anymore. You can spend the money on something else.' Raymond looked confused, and sat down next to the cross with the poem, the flowers, the origami frog and the cans of cheap dog food. The abandoned blue bag, already worried by the wind, was whipped up into the air. Raymond and the care assistant watched as it climbed higher and higher like a kite escaping into the clouds. Soon it had flown out of sight. Marcel came out in his wheelchair with another origami figure.

'A swan,' he said, and held it out on his hand for Raymond to place by the cross.

'Are you getting another dog?' he said, head on one side as he looked at the cans of food, but Raymond and the care assistant were still gazing up at the sky. Eventually the care assistant got out a packet of fags and passed them round.

'Turned into a clock, tumbled down a hill,' Raymond murmured, remembering a song, or a nursery rhyme, some tune he had overhead. 'Turned into a clock, tumbled down a hill.'

The First Time

Silence. I can hear the creak of cranes over King's Cross and the rumble of cars on the Euston Road, so it's a funny kind of silence. Feels like you should be here with me. You should be putting your head round the door with a drying up cloth in your hand and smiling the wonky smile you used on me when I was upset. But you're not here, so you don't, I imagine it instead. This place is too full of you. You're round every corner, in every cobweb and each bit of flaky paint in the bathroom, and your shape's still there on the bed and in the kitchen next to the sink making leek and potato soup. I sit down to eat my beans on toast and think about you as I push a mouthful of squashed beans and bread into my mouth.

Stop it stop it stop it, I tell myself. Slow down. Sex will make me feel better. I feel tense. I want to stop feeling tense. My erection hurts. My jeans are too tight. I stumble up from the table. I feel like Bananaman. I'm Eric and I've eaten the banana. Trying to keep my feet on the ground is all stupid when I'm this clever. Women in the street look at me because they want to have sex with me. The men are looking at me too. I walk faster. I hold my head higher. The sun breaks through the clouds just because I'm walking down the street. I see myself reflected in shop windows. I look great. Later I'm going to enrol at like some really big university, and they'll be pleased to have me. I'll probably win a prize. Forget about work. They don't care whether I turn up anyway. I go quickly down our road and onto York Street, and stop outside a shop called EZ Video. Upstairs are bedsits where the girls are.

'Mate,' I say. I'm standing in reception. It reminds me of the minicab office. 'Sort me out.' The guy behind the desk licks his teeth. I hand him some money and he passes me a pink ticket. I'm hopping from foot to foot like I need a toilet. I'm about to run upstairs holding my pink ticket when he reaches out and grabs my coat.

'Hey,' I say, wishing he would let go, hoping to calm him down. 'What's your name?'

'Mike,' he says. I prise his fingers from my collar. I can see he is on something strange from the expression he pulls.

'Whatever you're taking it ain't doing you much good,' I say. I'm getting impatient. 'I've got to go now, if you know what I mean.' I feel like I'm going to burst. I imagine bits of myself all over the reception; pink and red and yellow bits of exploded me.

'Try the new girl,' Mike says. 'Second floor. On the right.' The stair carpet is worn and smells damp. I run up and knock on the door. A young woman with long blonde hair answers. She has a sweet up and down accent like a thrush singing. She lets me into the bedsit. When I look into her face I feel calmer. She hasn't got the hard look in her eyes you expect. I can see things in those eyes. Pictures. Her cheeks are soft like little pillows. I run my hand over her face. She knocks it away.

'Ticket?' she says. I hand it over.

'Shower first.' The hot water makes me feel a bit better. I dry myself and drop the towel on the floor. I walk back into the room naked. She is lying on the bed in her underwear.

'What's your name?' she says.

'Harry,' I say. 'You?'

'My name is Sophia,' she says. She looks at me without smiling. I climb on top, put my hands either side of her shoulders. Her hair is spread out on the pillow around her. She looks like a mermaid. I don't touch her. I look into her face.

'What are you doing here?' I ask her.

'What are you doing here?' she says back. I shrug. I think about the weirdness of two strangers about to have sex, two people whose lives are crossing in that moment because of all the messed up things that have happened to bring them to this point.

'Sometimes I'm up. Sometimes I'm down. Today I'm up,' I say. I grin. 'I'm Superman today,' I add, in case she hasn't got it. I am still looking down on her. Her cheap black bra is frayed. It annoys me. I don't want frayed.

'Are you an angel?' I say.

'Whatever you want,' she says. She sounds bored.

'You haven't told me where you're from.' For some reason I want to talk and to look into her face for longer.

'Kiev. How long did you pay for?'

'Twenty minutes.' I sit back on my heels. She hands me a condom.

'Better hurry up or you'll have to pay more.'

'Can't we talk first?' I open the packet.

'OK. I'll ask you a question. Why do you have to get it here?' I roll the condom on. I hold it in place so it doesn't roll back up.

'My wife died.'

'Do you believe in God? Do you go to church?' she says. Sitting holding my dick, I suddenly get the feeling that I look like one of those water fountains of Eros pissing into a fish pond. An overgrown one. A monster. Not Superman. Not Bananaman. A prat. I sit back so I'm kneeling at the end of the bed.

'You're a prostitute,' I say, probably too defensively. 'Why are you telling me about church? You a preacher in your spare time?' Sophia shrugs.

'You said you wanted to talk.' Her hair isn't only blonde. There are tiny patches of auburn in it too. I think about it again: two strangers whose paths cross like lines on a map because things have happened to get them there. We're both the same, I think. It makes me honest.

'OK. Yeah I believe in God,' I say. 'I believe in life after death. Old lady downstairs from me? Medium, right?' I want to impress her. I don't know why.

'You talk to dead people with the lady next door?'

'Yeah,' I say. I take her knickers off. She lifts her legs up to help me. I did the medium thing once, I think, nothing happened *and* it freaked me out, but I make out to Sophia I don't care.

'So if you talk to dead people what does your wife think of you coming here?' she says, raising an eyebrow.

'Never asked.' Sophia smiles. I notice that her teeth are stained with tar.

'Tell me about the first time you met her,' she says. So I do.

❦

The first time I see her I am in my big coat, the one with the woodpecker logo. I sit next to a tree in the bird sanctuary with my binoculars. I put my hand on the bark. On one side it is soft and damp and mossy and on the other side it's dry and rugged. The morning smells new and the mist is hovering over the fields behind me like a ghost. I watch as the guy who has been stealing the eggs gets closer. He is wearing a balaclava. He hasn't seen me. He is carrying a ladder, the tosser. He stops and looks around, and then runs towards the tree where they are nesting. The police are ready, but we have to wait until he has got his hands on the eggs. He puts the ladder to the tree. He is about two hundred metres in front of me. I've got a clear view. He knows where the nest is because he goes straight for it. He has obviously been here before. He is up the ladder and groping about in the hole in the side of the tree. He's got a box with him. I can see it through my binoculars. He puts an egg inside it. My radio crackles. I wait for him to take one more, and then I whisper into the radio 'go', and the air is full of the sound of running police and he is surrounded. I come out from where I am hiding just as one of them shouts, 'Come down from the tree', and the birds nearby scatter and fill the air in panic. While he is arrested, a police car drives over the field towards us. I climb up the ladder. I have to reach in a long way to replace the eggs. A woman sits in the front of the police car. I smile at her. She smiles back. I don't realise how beautiful she is straight away. That doesn't happen until I look for a second time, but when it happens it hits me like a cliché in the chest.

I stand next to the police car, signing some papers. It is the electricity of her eyes that gets to me. It is like the time my dad tried to put some shelves up in our kitchen and moved the light switch and I got electrocuted. She looks at me, wide-eyed, as the egg thief is bundled into the back. I can feel myself being pulled towards her like I am a planet and she is a black hole. I try to keep my eyes fixed on the papers, but she winds the window down.

'I'm doing a thing,' she says. She shoves a card at me and I pocket it. 'Next week at City Books. You should come.' A policewoman shakes my hand.

'Good job,' she says and jumps in the car. The engine revs. Suddenly I am left alone with the birds.

❦

Sophia's pubes are shaved into a heart. A darker colour than the hair spread across the pillow. Nice touch, I think. What you pay for.

'That was the first time,' I say.

'So she was some kind of writer, your wife?' she says.

'Illustrator,' I say. The word sounds strange in my mouth, like over-chewed gum. 'But she came up with stories to go with the pictures.'

'Oh,' Sophia says. I do her slowly. When I look into her face she is blank. I wonder what she is thinking about. Halfway through, Mike bangs on the door.

'Time's up. You come out now or pay more.' When it is over, I feel stupidly embarrassed like the time I got caught wanking in the school toilets. Sophia puts her hand on my face.

'Come back again,' she says.

'Er, yeah. Whatever,' I say. I pull on my jeans. She lies on the bed in just her bra, watching me. I look back for a second. Yeah I will come back I think. I leave her twenty quid because I don't know how much Mike pays them.

I get on a train and I'm thinking about you. I can't help it. We go into a tunnel. I look at my reflection and my reflection looks back at me and I talk to you in my head. I'm not sure if I really am talking to you or if I am going mad, or if this is what the therapist's receptionist told me about: the psychological processes of grief. She ran the words together, like this: psychologicalprocessesovgrief, like she said it all the time. I don't want that because it would mean your voice in my head is not real. I think: yeah, but if the receptionist knows all the answers then why do I need to see the bloody therapist?

I tell you that I had sex with a prostitute called Sophia who had heart-shaped pubes and I wonder if you are listening. I want you to say 'Don't be stupid, of course I'm listening!' but you don't say anything. Then I try not to think about you, but that feels dangerous, like an astronaut too close to the sun. I try to provoke you into speaking:

'Why did I fall in love with you so easily?' You don't reply.

'What about those e-dating websites?' You don't reply.

'Am I the kind of person who gets dates on the internet?' I ask you.

'Probably not,' you say. When I hear your voice I get a spongy, soft feeling like eating a cake I'm not allowed to have and I know it will be bad for me. You watch me with your arms folded, but you don't say anything else. Silence. A creaky crane kind of silence.

The Smallest House in London

Outside Kings Cross Station, the autumn leaves are so squashed in the middle of Euston Road that they are only imprints of themselves, scattered like a pattern on a duvet, red, brown, yellow, green; ghosts of themselves, run over. I have just left Freddie at the Monastery. I want a bath. I want a drink. No, I want to be a drink; I want to know what it's like to be drunk. This is what happened.

I lived in a very small house. I was Freddie's fan mail co-ordinator. Freddie Lava is an ex boy-band-superstar. I was bigger than the house I lived in. I had to sit down, not stand up, and when I stretched out my arms, hug-like, I had to bend my elbows. On the walls, I had bookshelves, right up to the ceiling. I had a comfy chair with a rug in front of it and a fireplace. I had a duvet folded up, which I curled up on in the middle of the floor, like a cat, to sleep. Next to my chair, I had a microwave. I cooked my meals for one in it. Fish and vegetables or stew. Two minutes.

Stir. Three minutes. Done. The green numbers, which either told me the time or how long my food took to heat, glowed while I sat in my chair as if I had an exotic pet next to me in a basket.

When Freddie came round, I sat on the duvet and leant against the fireplace. I let him have the chair. I cooked a microwave meal for two. It took longer than five minutes. Chicken curry. I got naan bread sometimes too, pricked it with a fork, sprinkled it with water, thirty seconds. I had a small fridge behind my chair in front of the bathroom door. In the bathroom, there was a sink, a shower, and a toilet. In the bathroom, I could stand up, because it was an extension built years ago in a gap between two buildings. I went in there sometimes so I could stand up, turned on the light, listened to the fan, watched the tiny white tiles, and stretched. When we had sex, we did it standing up in the shower. It was awkward afterwards because it was difficult to move apart. There was a window high up in the bathroom, with a ledge where I kept things, soap, toilet paper, washing up liquid. I gazed at that ledge while he was on his knees in front of me. Those objects are erotically charged, seeing them out of context is like eating sherbet. Sometimes I dream about being inside the bathroom.

When I visited Freddie, I used to go and stand in his bathrooms. He had five of them. I ran my hand over the enamel and took off my socks so I could feel the black and white tiles with under floor heating. He had cats everywhere. Fluffy white and ginger ones, grey ones with green eyes. I don't know how many there were. They met me at the top of the stairs, in the garden near the big purple gladioli, in the golden-walled bathroom with the silver taps off the main landing. Freddie had a tiger once, but his PA got rid of it. Freddie's PA looked like a willowy version of Carrie Fisher, and like she might whip out a lightsaber at any moment. Her name was Anna, but everyone called her Freddie's PA.

Freddie's house was spread out over two square miles of landscaped garden in Holland Park. It had a still-blue swimming pool with big glass windows, and a fan with brown blades hanging from the ceiling, which was also still. His house went on for room after room after room. He could stretch out his arms wide, over and over, in every one of them. His ceilings were high, his hallways three times the size of my house. I liked to visit him. I felt like I was walking around a museum. I liked to wander up the stairs, hang around on the landing, poke my head into the bedroom cupboards, feel the carpet with my hand. When we ate together, burger and beer, on his wide lawn, all we could see was: his French doors onto the patio, his lawn, his trees, his bricks, his white garden table, his jug of water, and window after window after window.

Usually, I worked from home. The sacks of mail were delivered to my door, two at a time, because I couldn't fit any more in. I felt like Father Christmas, but in reverse. Freddie got cuddly toys, knickers, photos, love heart chocolates. I logged the gifts. If you sent an envelope, you got a signed photo. I packed the cuddly toys in a box. They went to social services. It was my idea, and Freddie's PA said it was good for his image. She got to keep the knickers (the clean ones). Postcards I stuck on my door or on my ceiling, so that when I looked up I could see places from all over the world. Freddie's PA got the chocolates too, because Freddie is lactose intolerant. Other than that, I saved what I could and took it to the charity shop down the road, the rest went to the dump.

I had a laptop, and control of the email account and the blog page. In the morning, I sorted through the emails, tweets and Facebook messages. I had a file for unusual requests. His lawyers made me keep a record. I was very organised. Everyone got a link to a ticket sales page and signed up to the email list, apart from the weird ones, who didn't get a reply. Unusual requests got a personal P.S. from me at the bottom of the email. *Freddie is sorry but he can't come for a hot air balloon ride with you.* Once I had sorted out the presents, put signed photos into envelopes, stuffed teddies into boxes, stuck postcards to my ceiling, stacked the chocolates and knickers for the PA, the courier arrived to take stuff back to the PR company's office and to bring more sacks.

In the afternoons, I sometimes went to the PR company's office, which took up the entire top floor of a warehouse somewhere that's impossible to find without the Docklands Light Railway. The company had some other minor clients, but the warehouse was laid out according to the big ones: Freddie Lava on one side, Shuffle, a neopunk girl band, in one corner, and Meathead on the other. Meathead are a Christian heavy metal outfit from the eighties, who still tour in Europe.

If I got left alone, and the phone went, I said *Freddie Lava's desk* quickly, as if I was busy, even if I wasn't. The woman who ran Freddie's desk was called Rum. I don't know if that is her real name. She had a cappuccino machine, so the air smelt of coffee, and a cheese plant that looked like it might take over one day and turn the whole warehouse into a jungle. Rum started work there when she left school. She had bunches and a pink T-shirt. She loved Freddie all her life. The walls in our side of the office were covered in posters of him grinning, or singing into a microphone.

If the phone was busy, you might have got through to Shuffle or Meathead instead. Behind the Meathead desk sat a man with long greasy hair and a permanent black T-shirt called Daz, like the washing powder, who almost never said anything. Shuffle had a bouncy-haired Cambridge graduate who would go down well in an episode of Scooby Doo. She was called Mandy, wore designer glasses, and was doing a part-time MPhil in Classical

Civilisations. She worked on the porno phone lines at night for extra money, and looked permanently tired. I was still there once when she had a call diverted to her mobile. Cornered on the phone by a fan wanting to know why she hadn't had a personal reply from Freddie, I heard Mandy crooning from the bathroom.

'I want to kiss your eyeballs,' she said. I think she might have been licking the phone.

At the time, none of them knew how small my house was. Once you were away from my house, you could imagine a sauna, a wide garden, a dressing room painted red, a horse in a paddock, a kitchen with all the gadgets, a mixer, a juicer, a squeezer, a toaster oven, a waffle griddle, a sandwich maker.

The day in question, Daz (greasy hair, black T-shirt) sat sulkily at his desk, staring at his phone, Rum (pink T-shirt, bunches) chewed her gum viciously and laughed. Mandy (bouncy hair, glasses) came through the arch between Shuffle and Freddie Lava.

'Coffee,' she said. It wasn't a question, it was a requirement. You had to drink coffee to talk to her. Once I went to the warehouse after dark to pick up some more signed photographs. When I went in, the alarm wasn't on, and the light was still on in Shuffle's part of the office. Through two arches, I could see Mandy on the phone with one foot on the desk. She was looking out at something in front of her. I had to go right through to the Shuffle office before I saw that she was reading Tarot cards.

'The Sun,' she said into the phone. 'You're going to be very happy soon, think positive, do something nice for yourself, take a holiday, somewhere hot.' She looked up at me, chewing her pencil, and put the card down on the desk. It didn't have a sun on it. It was a picture of a man with lots of swords in his back. I stared at her.

'I try to make them happy,' she said. 'Coffee.'

So, on the day in question, Mandy passed round the coffee. I sipped the froth on my cappuccino, secretly wishing I could touch her bouncy hair, while she told me about Athens and the foundation of democracy. I held a print out of an email in my hand, thinking I was going to log it in the lawyer's file under weirdo:

I've had enough. This is the only way out. You can have the bloody house. It was sent from a Gmail address and wasn't signed.

The first time I went to Freddie's house, Pete (he's the butler) showed me into the reception room, a large square lounge with a smart fireplace and a glass table, which held the first three parts of Freddie's autobiography: *Freddie Lava: My Life in Words, Lava: the Early Days* and *The Freddie Phenomenon*. A large TV on the wall played Freddie videos. The table also held an ashtray, which looked as though it had never been used, and a vase of white flowers. I sat in the arm chair and watched TV. When Freddie came down to meet me with his PA, he looked me up and down and his PA asked me questions:

'What was the name of Freddie's third solo album?'

'Cheese Maniac.' She circled me, and picked up the ashtray as if it were a beautiful object. She passed it from hand to hand. Freddie sat down in a chair by the French door and put his head in his hands.

'Have you done this kind of thing before?' said his PA.

'I used to work for Children's BBC, sorting birthday requests. Before that, the Post Office doing letters to Santa.'

'Fine. Have we got your CV?'

'Yes.' I had already had the interview at the PR company with Daz the Meathead guy. He was some kind of managing director, although you wouldn't know it. It was more of a tea and chat than an interview.

'I got cake,' Daz had said, passing me a plate of Mr

Kipling's French Fancies.

Meeting Freddie was the last stage in the selection process. Freddie was still in the armchair by the door. Occasionally he would moan as if there were too much in the world to think about.

'Is he OK?' I said.

'What?' said the PA. I nodded at Freddie.

'Oh yes. He's fine. He's composing.' After that I imagined him writing songs in that armchair with his head in his hands, although he had a studio in the basement of the house where no-one was allowed to go.

'You'll do,' said the PA. 'When can you start?'

The police asked me later if I called Freddie my boyfriend, and I said no. Freddie turned up one afternoon and asked to talk. We talked. I think he liked how I had never heard of him before I applied for the job. His fame didn't impress me. The wine helped, I told them. We ended up in the shower.

I drained my coffee. I was about to show the email about the house to Mandy and Rum. I remember that moment as if it were frozen in time: Daz had his feet on the desk and was playing Candy Crush on his phone. The phone rang.

'Freddie Lava's desk,' Rum said. She froze as she listened, then looked like she might throw up. We waited, blank-faced, for her to tell us what had happened. It seemed like several minutes, but was probably a couple of seconds. I crumpled the email into a ball in my hand. The tension was too much and I needed to destroy something.

'Freddie,' she said. Daz, Mandy and I did various versions of 'What the fuck?' until she told us.

'He's dead.' Rum dropped the phone and shrieked at it, like it had killed Freddie and had turned on her. Mandy tried to calm her down. I stared at them both, totally unable to believe what she had said. That was when Daz picked up the receiver and the PA told him what had happened.

Cocaine and whisky were involved. Heart-attack after too much masturbation. The rest of that day was full of interviews with the police, each of us in turn. We failed, absolutely, to keep it out of the press. The headlines ranged from 'Pop Star Wanked Himself to Death' through 'Lava's Night of Shame', to 'Hedonism's Ironic Twist: Lava is a victim of his own superficial world', and even, in the *New Scientist*, 'The Lava Phenomenon: Negated Introspection and the Narcissism Complex'.

❦

I arrived early. From the ruined chapel, I followed the spiral staircase, which was covered in ivy, down into the garden. I could smell lavender and mint. The garden was square, and laid out like a maze with a tree in the centre, although the tallest plant reached only my knees. On the staircase, you could see the patterns from above, like God. Once you were standing in the gardens they disappeared.

I met Freddie after I had wandered around the garden for a while. I found him waiting for me in the ruined chapel, sitting near the back. He looked shocked and dishevelled, like I had asked him a question and he didn't have the answer.

'Thanks for leaving me the house,' I said. He closed his eyes. The air around him was still and holy. Browning leaves circled on the floor next to the memorial slabs; part of the roof was missing, and a thick bramble was snaking its way in through the window. The cold air blew around our heads while we prayed as if the spirits were listening and carrying our thoughts up another flight of spiral stairs, this time invisible ones, to wherever heaven is. Some late wasps circled my head drunkenly. They swam slowly in the holy air, ready to die. Freddie still had his eyes closed. I closed mine too. While I tried to pray I imagined the brambles creeping further into the church, growing around the brown pews, hugging the pulpit, the statue of Jesus raising his hands, growing around where we sat.

I had had enough of listening to spirits. I needed something to warm up my hands: hot chocolate, a baked potato to hold, a warm apple pie, anything. I had spotted a café on the other side of the garden, part of a modern building with a roof. That must be where they all lived, I thought.

'I want to go to the café and warm up,' I said. Freddie got up and didn't open his eyes until he was standing. Then he shook himself as if he were shaking off the last words of prayer. I wondered who he had been praying for. I hoped that he prayed for himself. I hope he said 'Bless me, bless me, bless me' over and over and over, like he couldn't stop sneezing. I hope he said 'give me honey, flowers, pages, sunshine, love' like a mantra, then I wondered if he had prayed for me.

'What did you pray for?' I asked as we went down the spiral stairs into the garden. He looked surprised, like I had asked him to spell out his birthday candle wishes for every one of the fifty years of his life. A pigeon stirred behind us. It frightened a squirrel who dropped from the tumbledown wall of the chapel next to the garden stairs and scurried away into the sunshine.

'I don't pray for things,' Freddie said then, as if I would never comprehend but he had to tell me anyway. He wore the frustrated but vaguely superior expression of people who knock on your door and ask you if you have found the Lord, only Freddie looked more determined than that. Steely, almost.

'Do you pray for people,' I said, 'instead of things, I mean?' hoping I had understood him. We were in the middle of the garden, the ruined chapel behind us on its own bank of earth, like a beacon. Freddie was walking too slowly. Ponderously. I saw the squirrel again, leaping along a stone wall towards a leaning tree branch. I hoped Freddie would say that he prayed for himself and for me and for world peace. Peace would have been a standard thing, I thought, looking up at the tree. Praying for peace is safe, not specific enough to be dangerous.

'I think about leaves,' Freddie said with a sigh, like he had to be brave to say it. The autumn sun shone down on the square maze garden. We walked around it. I tried to pick up the pace because I was cold; Freddie resisted.

'Today,' he said, 'I thought about brown leaves.' I bent down and picked up a brown leaf.

'Like this one?' I said. Maybe he would think it was spiritual. He took it from me.

'Yes,' he said. 'In the Spring, I think about the colour green.'

'Do you say "Dear God" and "Amen" and all that stuff?' I said, sniffing the lavender, which filled my head so much I couldn't think of anything else for a second.

'Dear God, leaf, Amen. Dear God, Green, Amen,' I said, trying it out. He put his head on one side.

'No,' he said, hesitating slightly. 'Not like that.' I got lost in the smell of lavender again for a moment.

'I make up a name,' Freddie added when I didn't reply. I could have been in a lavender pond with my head under water.

'What like Doris or Bob?' I said. He hesitated again and crumpled up his face as if it were a hard question.

'Dear Bob, Green, Amen,' I said, moving on to the dog roses. Freddie walked next to me. His arm brushed mine. I put my hand on it, as an experiment. He didn't pull away.

'Sometimes I just think about leaves generally,' he said. We watched the path in front of us where several leaves tumbled over and over like children.

'I don't say Bob,' he said.

'Why not?' I said.

'It's a stupid name for a God. Have you ever heard of a God called Bob?' I thought about it. I conjured up all the

Gods' names I could. They were mostly Greek: Artemis, Apollo, Dionysus, Zeus, Poseidon.

'You're right,' I said. 'Sorry.' We carried on walking, past some spiky pink and white flowers and a stone bench that said *All Manner of Things Shall Be Well – Julian of Norwich*. I looked it up on my phone. According to Wikipedia, Julian of Norwich was bricked up in a small room in a church, and Julian wasn't even her name, so it was unlikely that all things were well. Freddie stood waiting for me, gazing into the distance.

'You don't say Apollo or,' I said, trying to start the conversation again, but distracted for a moment by an advert for shoes that popped up on my phone.

'No. I told you,' Freddie said. 'I make it up.'

'What like Haberjab-Juberjob or Wakachuck?' I slipped the phone into my pocket; it was making me lose my train of thought.

'Don't be stupid,' Freddie said, looking about him to see if anyone had heard. They hadn't. Freddie pulled up his brown hood. His face got lost inside it. I played with my feet for a bit, scuffing them on the stony path in front of Julian's bench. I had tears in my eyes because Freddie had called me stupid, but he didn't notice.

'Anyway, you were praying too,' Freddie said, encouragingly, acting for a moment like he was teaching Sunday School. The leaves were still tumbling.

'Yes, but I just said the usual.'

'What do you mean by that?'

'You know. "Dear God (things I want) Amen." I didn't know you were allowed to make up names.' I could hear my voice getting higher. I was upset. I waved my arms when I said 'make up names'. Freddie looked me directly in the face for the first time since we met, and I think he saw how worried my eyes had become.

'Come on. Let's go to the café,' Freddie said. We carried on walking.

'What would Bob be God of?' I said. 'If there was a God Bob.' Freddie shrugged.

'Ordinary stuff.'

'Car radios?' I said, which made Freddie laugh, so I carried on.

'Pavements? Wheelie bins?' I looked around for inspiration. 'Guttering, plant pots, crisp packets, bricks.'

'I'm cold,' Freddie said.

'So am I,' I said. 'That's what I've been trying to tell you. I was cold before I even got here.' Freddie turned to face me, and took my hands in his. From a distance we must have looked like we were in a sci fi movie, him with his brown hood up; me, well, I was an extra, and I hadn't got changed into my robes yet.

'What did you pray for?' Freddie asked me.

'Do you think God Bob is pissed off that no-one prays to him?' I asked.

'Answer the question.' My eyes filled with tears again. I tried to change my face so Freddie couldn't read it.

'I prayed for you,' I said. 'I mean, I want you back. What did you do it for? Why did you pretend to die and come here? Why did you leave the house behind? What about the cats? The studio? Why did you leave me behind?' I said it all in a rush, like I was being sick and words were coming out instead of mashed up vegetables. Freddie took my face in his hands. I loved it when he did that. It made me want to grab him and roll around on the ground with him. I tried to kiss him. He pulled away. I wiped my face with my sleeve and looked around to distract myself.

I gazed up at the ruined chapel behind us and the spiral stairs. The plaque on the wall next to us said The Cellar Garden. Built in the ruins of the church cellar after it was exposed by a bomb in 1941.

'I didn't know churches had cellars.'

'The monks were making illegal cider under the chapel in the vaults instead of burying people there.'

'Where did they put the bodies?'

'Which bodies?'

'The ones they were supposed to bury.'

'No-one knows.'

'And the monks had to leave?'

'When the chapel was bombed in the second world war, yes. Some of them had sweethearts already on the outside, and they got married. One of them started a pub.'
I looked around at the garden, seeing it in a new light.

'And this is where they did it?' I said.

'Yes,' Freddie said, satisfied with his explanation. 'I prayed for you at the end,' he said.

'Before Amen?' I asked. He put his hands on my shoulders.

'I didn't say Amen,' he said, like it was important.

'You have to or it won't work,' I said automatically.

'You went to a weird kind of Sunday school.'

'What did you say about me?' I asked.

'I thought about you.'

'Like the leaves?'

'Yes. I thought about your face those times in the shower.'

'And what's going to happen now you've done that?' I asked.

'Prayers aren't just for making things happen,' he said.

'Can we get hot chocolate now?' I said. We moved further along the path, holding hands. I wasn't sure if monks were supposed to hold hands, if they weren't allowed to kiss, but we did it anyway. Finally, we got to the café and I clutched the cup of hot chocolate to warm my hands and let the steam heat my face.

'I didn't know about that,' I said.

'What?' Freddie asked.

'About praying and thinking things. About leaves, bombs, cider, God Bob, spiral stairs, lavender, squirrels and dog roses. Are you going to tell me why you did it?'

'I couldn't take it anymore,' Freddie said, squinting at me from beneath his brown hood. 'The constant self-indulgence.'

'So you got your PA to pretend you died? Isn't that a little extreme?'

'I didn't want anyone to find me. How's the house? How are the people?'

'Fine. We're thinking of running courses for apprentice musicians. Daz, Rum, Pete and me. Mandy is on an archaeological dig somewhere in Greece. Your PA found a job working for the chief exec of a sanitary protection company. We turned the small house into a museum.' Freddie nodded. He seemed pleased.

'And the cats?'

'Fine.' I sipped my hot chocolate. 'Why say you masturbated to death? Turned you into a bit of a laughing stock.'

'It was symbolic,' he said. I must have looked blank.

'Self-gratification,' he said. 'That's what I was leaving behind. I literally died from it.'

'You figuratively died from it,' I said. I had it on one of those grammar nerd mugs I saw on Facebook.

'No. The old me *literally* died from too much self-gratification. This is the new me. Plus, the headlines made me laugh.'

'Do you fancy a bit of self-gratification now?' I said. 'Where's your room?'

'Don't be stupid,' he said. 'I'm a monk.'

'One last time? Just to say goodbye?' Freddie shook his head.

'I have to go now,' he said. He stood up.

'Do you actually believe in all this … this stuff?' I said. I was going to swear, but seeing as I was in a monks' cafeteria I decided against it. I gestured to the rest of the cafeteria, which, admittedly, seemed substantial enough without the need to believe in it. Salt and pepper. Wooden chairs. A sunflower in a vase on every table.

'Believe? There's nothing to believe in,' Freddie said, smiling. 'You can see it all right in front of you.'

'Right.'

'Bye,' Freddie said. 'By the way, there's a wasps' nest in the garden at the House. Be careful.'

'Is it a sign?' I said. 'That my prayer's been answered?'

'Probably not.' With that Freddie went through a door on the other side of the café, which I imagined lead to the rest of the monks' quarters, and didn't look back.

I retraced my footsteps through the cellar garden, towards the falling-to-pieces chapel. A gate we hadn't been through led to an overgrown patch of land. I went through the gate. Dandelions, bindweed, holly bushes and nettles grew all over the place. On the far side sat a stone trough, with a hose coming from one end. I went over to it and peered inside, hoping to find somewhere to make a wish. As I was looking into the brown water, I heard footsteps behind me. I turned to find a monk wearing the same brown hooded robe and sandals as Freddie.

'What are you doing?' he said.

'Just looking.'

'You're trespassing,' he said. I thought he was pretty rude for someone who was supposed to be holy.

'Do you know about God Bob?' I asked him. He looked at me as if I were mad.

'This part is closed to the public.'

'I'll tell you about God Bob.'

'Leave, please,' he said. Then I saw two big stone jars by the hedge.

'Are you making cider?' I asked.

'Yes,' said the monk. 'If you want some, we sell it in the gift shop.'

'Where's that?'

'The other side of the chapel,' he said. 'Now sod off.' I went reluctantly back through the cellar garden and up the stairs. I found the gift shop, but they only sold post-cards.

When I got home nothing had happened apart from the kitchen clock had stopped, at 12:15. I looked on the internet to find out if anything had happened at precisely that time, like someone dying or being born, that kind of thing, but it didn't say.

Unusual Places

The Collage Garden

I walk through the low-ceilinged cloisters, with their rough white walls, and into the College Garden. It's an early autumn day. Bronze leaves already decorate the grass, like the trees have been scattering confetti. The garden is in a courtyard, and we're surrounded by red houses. Nearby buses sigh, and from an open window tinny music plays. Aeroplanes rumble overhead, and traffic creaks like an old funfair; long tuba sounds and high-pitched violin, while the wind makes the leaves sing, round ones, five fingered ones, tiny, private church-like ivy, fir needles, all singing. A helicopter beats its way through the sky. In front of me a jet of white water makes patterns and sounds like a crowd cheering. Leaves tumble over themselves in the wind, like children running. There's a palm tree, too, and a feathery grey delicate thing next to it, and a small tree with fat friendly fingers.

I sit down next to the herb garden where the monks used to make cures for the sick out of rosemary, lavender and fennel. The tall trees in front of me look wise. Their grave heads nod with long green wigs and, further up, their branches mingle. A woman with a baby goes past, plus three tourists and a man on a mobile phone. The tourists stare at me. I try to pretend it's because they are tourists and I'm a sculpture, but it's what people usually do. Either that or they pretend not to see.

'Funny face,' one of them says and turns away.

I'm wearing my anorak. It's green. I've done the buttons up. Now that we're on the cusp of autumn the air feels chilly. I can smell the powder I put on this morning, thick pink powder from a puff that I sniff like a security blanket, like a lover's trinket, every morning. I like thick powder. I like the smell under my nose. The powder is to cover up the scars, although sometimes I think it makes them stand out more.

I turn and spot some bamboo under one of the tall trees and think of pandas. Later, when I wash my face in front of the mirror and the pink water drips from my hands I will remember pandas. Did I see pandas today? I'll ask myself. No, I'll say back, I saw bamboo. I heard a baby cry. I heard buses pass and traffic like a funfair. I saw trees in wigs and a loud fountain.

Now I'm looking at the tree bark. I like how it is a single colour at a glance and different colours when you look close. I like how it is lumpy. It reminds me of elephant skin, wrinkled and patchy. I touch my powdered face, and the tip of my finger turns pink. I think about how, if that man on his mobile phone sat down next to me, I could press my fingertip onto the palm of his free hand and mark him, so that wherever he went he would have a pink print on his hand. Until he washed his hand, or perhaps he would pass it on when he shook hands with someone.

The traffic moans like an animal saying find me I am lost. I imagine what it would be like to climb the biggest tree, to sit in its raised hand where the trunk divides into branches. I imagine what I would look like shimmying up the trunk in my green anorak, then I could sit and look at the bench where I am now. I go over to the foot of the tree and look up at the branches. Suddenly, I am surrounded by green leaves, as if the whole world were made of them. If I carry on looking up, I can imagine that there is nothing else anywhere except me and the leaves. I turn around to find out who is watching. The curtain in one of the windows of the red house away to my left moves gently, and I see a child's face. She has a finger in her mouth and her eyes are wide. She looks sad. I wonder why she has to stay inside. I put my foot onto the trunk. I think she knows what I am going to do. She is staring intently now. The woman with the baby sits down by the fountain with her back to me. The man on the mobile phone struts up and down, up and down, waving one arm, like he's conducting. The tourists turn and point at me.

I wrap my arms around the trunk and lift up my other foot, press my knees hard so I can hold on. I am amazed because suddenly I am off the ground. I let one knee loose and push my foot up a bit more, then the other. I am hugging the tree tight now, halfway up the trunk. I am like one of those hippies: the ones that protest about motorways. I don't look down. I keep on going up. I get to the first branch and pull myself up further. It is easier now. All I have to do is pull up my legs, reach up to the higher branches, and again, and one final shove up and there I am sitting in the palm of the tree, branches shooting off all around me. The leaves hang like I am in a jungle. I swing my legs to and fro and laugh. I look at the child in the window and wave, then down at the pointing tourists, and across to the bench where I was sitting. I look over at the noisy fountain, the woman and her baby, the strutting man on the mobile phone, at the patch of bamboo and the palm tree. It feels like I am in the bit of the tree where it thinks. The tree thinks: someone sitting in my branches;

not the cat again, heavier than the cat, an oldish woman; funny face; powder on it to make it look better. Yes, the tree thinks, that's OK.

I can hear the air rustling around in the leaves like it is looking for the best ones to throw to the ground. Only a few leaves are yellow. Most are still green. The tourists are taking photos of the fountain. Only the girl at the window is watching now. The woman with the baby stares into space. She's eating a sandwich while the baby is asleep. Pigeons gather around her feet. She doesn't notice. I press my hand against my face and my palm comes away powdery. I press my hand against the tree: not a perfect handprint, but I can make out the fingers and the puffy parts of my palm. A woman in a creamy coloured cardigan walks past below with a cup of tea in a polystyrene cup. My mouth feels ready for a cup of tea.

I push my feet out so they're over the lower branch and swing myself down carefully. Then I sit down on it and hug the tree again. I wrap myself round it like a monkey and squeeze my knees together. I look up at the window. I used to be a gymnast, I want to tell her, but I can't because the windows are far away across the lawn. I think I see her smile before she moves back from the window, and I don't see her anymore. I shuffle down the tree and land on the grass again. I sit down with my back to the tree and get my breath back.

When I get home I think of pandas and tea in polystyrene cups and biscuits. I think of shadows dancing on the grass; I think of leaves running and lost animals; I think of noisy fountains; I think of the sad face at the window.

Kensington Gardens

I came to the park today where the thick hedges have been trimmed to look like giant sandcastles. First I sit in the white café next to a table of cakes and freesias in a glass that smell like water and sugar, piles of strawberries and scones, and statues raising a hand to their heads. I drink tea from a blue and white cup and look out at the rows of hedges that line the path. There is a tree with red branches just outside the window. It could be made of feathers. Afterwards I walk round the lake and watch the geese and smooth white swans. The wind is teasing the surface with light fingers like it is turning cards over blue, white, blue, white. I'm wearing my green anorak. I powdered my face carefully, covering the scars, breathing in the scent like I am one of those people on drugs. I can smell it as I walk past the lake and look at the swans. Then I stand in the middle of the path and let the toddlers and the people on bikes go past me on either side.

I stop suddenly. I go back on myself and approach the edge of the lake. The geese come up to me in case I start eating sandwiches and drop crumbs. I can still smell the flowers from the white café. Now I can smell the water, too, and goose shit. Have you noticed how big tea leaves turn when you pour water on them? I noticed it today. They look like the broken bits of leaf that might float in a puddle. I guess they *are* broken bits of leaf.

When I go home today, I will remember piles of scones and strawberries, leaves that swell and could float in a puddle, flowers and goose droppings. I take off my anorak. I unbutton it slowly. Someone starts scattering crisps on the ground. The geese waddle towards them. I think about pandas, elephants and sitting in a jungle. I have a pink and blue and green and white dress on, with flowers. It has white plastic buttons up the front. I can feel the powder as it clutches the hair on my top lip. I can taste my lipstick. It tastes of Mr Kipling's icing. I undo my dress one button at a time. Now I am in my tights and pants and my cream bra and my pumps. The white ones. The man who scattered his crisps for the geese stands, crisp packet upturned in his hand, mouth open. It's cold. The autumn air rushes in between my legs and under my arms.

In cafés that smell of freesias, I think, randomly, the waiter should bring you top ups of boiling water. I think back to my milk-clouded tea, and my silver tea-strainer and how small the holes were. What would it be like to wriggle through one of those holes? The things that tea can do that I can't. I think all these things while the crisp-packet man and the geese watch and my arms get cold. I notice how flabby they are, how pink and soft, like bread dough. Then I jump into the lake.

I am glad that I know how to swim, that I'm not afraid of water. I can smell the weeds much more strongly now. I dip my head under the water: to see if I can open my eyes. Everything looks cloudy. What if the world always looked like this? When I reach the surface again, a small crowd of people is watching. When I wipe my eyes, I can feel the powder smearing across my cheeks. I raise my arms and swim a few strokes. It feels good. I do it again. A swan flaps its wings in alarm and gets out of my way. When I climb out again, someone has found a towel for me, like we're in a film. Where do towels come from in emergencies? Or maybe it is a blanket. Maybe someone has a red checked picnic blanket and they wrap it round my shoulders. Someone else awkwardly hands me my dress and coat like they are giving me flowers. I put them on and walk back to the café, my hair dripping.

I sit at the same table as before and order more tea. When it comes I lift the lid off the teapot so I can watch the leaves growing bigger.

❦

Roman Amphitheatre

The orange flowers tumbled out of the window boxes like children running from a pillow fight. You said you'd meet me outside the Roman Amphitheatre and that you would bring coffee. You told me to walk across the wobbly bridge. I guess people didn't like it wobbling because they thought they were going to get thrown into the river. When you told me to walk over it, I imagined splashing, inflatable life savers, crumbling stratifications, but it doesn't wobble any more.

When you said amphitheatre, I imagined crowds of seats, dust, shouting and sand, and I remembered the other two times I've seen a Roman amphitheatre. The first: when I climbed up to the stadium at Delphi and the ground was pink. I imagined chariots and heat. It was so hot at Delphi I could hardly move. Now, in the autumn chill, I imagine it again, climbing uneven stone, footstep after footstep, following your heels, watching them rise and fall, the sky like a blue oven all around us, and we're trapped inside it, my thighs aching, mildly disappointed that we haven't figured out exactly where the oracle lived because you wanted to ask a question. When we turn around, we can see Apollo's temple and the gleaming white coach that brought a pack of American tourists who are climbing the steep path at the same time as us with blank faces. It's too old and too hot and no-one has told us about the future. I look around at the sky again. Nothing. I think about beer.

The second time, we argued in Arles when a short French man took us on a tour. There used to be bull fighting. There were wooden seats; we walked underneath them. At the time, I tried hard to imagine lions and gladiators, but all I could think about was our argument still ringing in my head, and when I thought about it again crossing the wobbly bridge in the autumn I could feel the injustice of it in the pit of my stomach, though I had no idea what the argument was about. I remember standing by the seats looking down at the preserved arena, hearing our words echoing, missing you.

I remember things in pieces: Pythia, I think, priestess, snake woman. Was the oracle in a hole in the ground like a mouth? I'd like to ask it a question now. Bricks, steps, red dust, pancake sky, oven hot, gladiator wheels, dead chickens, our argument. I can remember that we were near the café where Van Gogh painted the Yellow Café, and that the owners had painted it yellow to make it look like the painting, but if you look closely you'll see that he was painting the lamplight, not the colour of the walls.

After I've said yes, yes, I'll cross the wobbly bridge and meet you, yes, bring coffee, yes, the amphitheatre, yes, bring the dog, yes, bring a match, a pen, a flower, bring a whole bag full of things; after I've said yes, I realise I don't know where the amphitheatre is. It seemed so substantial when you said it: like everyone in London knows where it is, like, don't be stupid, it's as famous as the Globe, Trafalgar Square, the London Eye.

'Don't you remember?' I say to myself in my pretend conversation, the one I often have with you. 'Don't you know where it is?' I close my eyes and try to picture it on the bank of the Thames, with flags, red dust, American Tourists, a white coach, a small French tour-guide, Apollo, Pythia, blank faces, ice cream, a painting by Van Gogh, an argument. I walk up and down the South Bank looking for it because that's where the other theatres are, right? I can't phone you and tell you I don't know where it is. That would be like saying I can't remember the location of St. Paul's Cathedral or what it looks like. I imagine you with coffee, dog, and the other things in a bag: flowers, cards, maybe your camera, to take a photo of us. I walk all the way from the London Eye to the Globe, past the second-hand bookstall and the skateboarders who echo round my head like we're in a cave. I have tears in my eyes when I think of you: camera, dog, coffee, with the round walls behind you, Pythia, the lions, the oracle (where we would have asked), the blue sky like an oven. I look up at the big chimney of the Tate Modern and say a prayer. You'll be there by now. Maybe if I can talk to God in my head, He'll talk to you – like a go between, and He can tell you where I am. Or maybe I can get straight through to you, just with thought waves. I screw up my eyes tight.

'I'm here,' I say in my head. 'Here, here, here. Can you see me?' When I look up I see a woman in a red two-piece suit, auburn hair and strange pixie black shoes, sitting next to me. I notice that I've sat down on a bench next to the Thames. She is holding an expensive-looking black coat, a bag with two coffee cups in it, and a handbag. She takes out an apple and eats it. I worry that she will get in the way of my prayer. I get up and lean on the railing and look down at the water. I screw up my eyes again.

'I'm here,' I say. Imagine being trapped in a cave with skateboarders: the hollow sound would knock around your head. It's dark. There's no way out. Maybe there is a way out but you can't find it.

I wonder if you've got the dog on the lead and how you're managing to hold the coffee with the other things you've brought. On the other hand, that dog would follow you without the lead, or rather, follow your ankles, hugging them like he's made of Velcro. He thinks your ankles are you. He thinks you consist mainly of your feet to about half way up your calves, and sometimes your face and hands. The hands that get his dinner and fold his ears back each evening with the sound of the TV in the background. They are separate things: feet, ankles, calves, hands, face. So you don't have to bring the lead. He'll hug your ankles, trying to trip you up all the way. I imagine you sitting down and tipping the bag out in front of you, like you did once that time we went camping, to see if you had brought the torch. You had brought it. You never forget anything. You go around your flat, throwing things into that bag: books, carrots, keys, lipstick, bus pass, torch, map, anything you can find.

I smile at the thought of the tent we put up together. I look around me as if there might be a sign any minute: the

Oracle might open up in the ground beside me. Or maybe the amphitheatre is just behind me and I've missed it. I think about the coffee you have bought. It'll be going cold. I decide to go back to the Tate and buy myself a coffee. At least it will be hot. I think about how it will smell. I think about the bitter taste. I think about pouring the milk in, one portion at a time, and stirring with a wooden stick. I'm sitting on one of the comfy chairs with my coffee, thinking about the stadium in Delphi, when my mobile phone rings. I look at the screen. It's you. I panic for a moment. What will I say? I got held up. Of course I know exactly where you are. I answer after I've let it ring a few times. I hear the dog.

'Where are you?' you say, trying to keep the argument, the one I can still feel in my stomach, out of your voice.

'I'm having coffee in the Tate gallery,' I say.

'Oh,' you say. 'Have you been to look at the paintings?'

'Not yet,' I say. 'But I might.'

'You're late,' you say.

'I won't look at the paintings. I'll come now. I'm sorry.'

'Good,' you say. 'You know how to get here, right?'

'Right,' I say. I gulp down my coffee and run down the stairs and out of the main door. I screw up my eyes and promise myself that next time I will look at all the paintings. I realise how serious it is to promise God something, imagining myself on judgement day.

'You could go into Heaven but,' (unrolling a scroll), 'you promised to look at all the paintings in the Tate Gallery.'

'I'll go back,' I say out loud. 'Give me another chance.' A woman walks past me. Her perfume smells flowery. I watch her take photos for a while. I feel her perfume sinking into my stomach where the argument sits. I wonder if God will give me another chance or not. If I say, 'Just let me go back to London for one day.' I'll go to all the galleries. The National, the Royal Academy, both Tates, the

Courtauld. I'll spend the whole day. I'll find out where the Amphitheatre is. One more day and I'll be waiting for you instead. It'll be me with the coffees and books about Van Gogh paintings and a bag full of flowers. I'll wait for you. I'll put perfume on. When you arrive with your dog at your heels, you'll unwrap the gingerbread you have in your pocket, in foil, and I'll pass you the coffee.

'Amphitheatre,' I'll say, pronouncing as many letters as possible. You collect amphitheatres. I'll collect them with you. Just on that day I'll collect them. I'll buy a new camera, and go all over London. My phone rings again. It's you.

'You don't know where it is, do you?' you say.

'No.' You sigh. I can hear how frustrated you are.

'See the bridge?' you say.

'The wobbly one?'

'Yes.'

'Go over that.' I walk towards it. You wait.

'See St Paul's?' you say.

'Yes.'

'OK. I'll meet you there.'

'Did you buy coffee?' I ask you.

'No. Not yet. I need one.'

'Glad you didn't buy one,' I say, trying to sound cheerful. 'It would have gone cold.'

You've brought your collection of amphitheatre postcards with you. You have bags stuffed inside your bag. The dog is bouncing excitedly next to us. We sit on the steps that Charles and Diana walked up and look at them. You hand them to me one at a time. Your hands are cold. I look at each picture. Some I've been to with you. I recognise them. Some you've collected on your own. You point out the architectural features, how round the walls are, how many seats there are inside, how many people were killed when it was restored.

'I'll buy you coffee,' I say eventually. You kiss me on the

cheek. You smell of soap. Lavender soap. I like it. I imagine washing my hands in it. I know which soap it is. It's the one with the bits in it that you bought from the expensive shop; the place where you can get honeycomb soap, marmalade soap, lemon blessing with basil leaf face scrub and body lotion. I like going in and poking my finger into the different pots. You kiss me again. It is very romantic: kissing on the steps of St. Paul's cathedral.

'You didn't want to go,' you say.

'Where?'

'The amphitheatre.'

'Don't be stupid. I love amphitheatres.'

'Admit it,' you say, and you put your arms round me until I'm laughing so much my eyes are watering.

'Admit it,' you say. You're leaning over me now. I can see all the details of your face. The dog has his muzzle on your knee. Once you had to put him inside a zip up bag for five minutes to smuggle him into a theatre in Athens. He hasn't forgiven you. Whenever he sees a sports bag with a zip, he hides. You were so sorry that you let him sleep under the covers at the bottom of your bed for two weeks, until you found muddy paw prints on your duvet. At least he got to stand next to you on the stage in the Greek theatre. You spread out your arms, and I laughed at both of you and took a photo before the old Greek woman came out of the booth to tell us off.

'OK. I admit it,' I say. Then you kiss me on the lips and I can taste your lipstick. It tastes powdery and fruity, like sweets; the sort my Auntie gave me once.

'Did you bring me some flowers?' I say.

'Yes.' You rummage in a blue plastic bag and pull out a sunflower. I hold the rough stalk and look into the big battered face, at the way the brown seeds curl.

'It's lovely,' I say. 'I have no idea where the amphitheatre is, by the way.' You grin at me and take me by the hand, and we run, you leading the way along the street so people have to move out of our way. The dog is yapping behind us. We turn the corner twice. I'm out of breath but we keep going, over the road. A clock chimes and a group of road diggers stop to watch us.

'Promised God I would look at paintings,' I say, between breaths.

'I know,' you say.

'How do you know?'

'He told me.'

'Aha,' I say. You pull me along the road past a snack bar, a health parlour and a map shop.

'How do you know He's a He?' I say.

'What?' you say. We cross another road. We're going so fast that my chest hurts.

'She then,' you say. 'She told me.'

'Couldn't you tell by her voice?' I say.

'What?'

'Her voice. Whether She was a man or a woman.'

'Could have been either,' you say enigmatically. You pull me up a side street, and suddenly we're in the middle of a grey and white square. Three posh cars are parked on the far side. You pull me into the middle and finally let go of my hand.

'Here we are,' you say, raising your arms like you do. Your bag is swinging at your elbow and you look like a statue in fancy dress. I glance quickly around me, wondering if this is a trick.

'Where?' I say. You tie the dog to a bench, and take me inside one of the buildings, past some paintings, and down some stairs into the basement.

'Do you think those paintings will do? Those ones we saw on the way in here? For God I mean?' But now we are underground. You stand in the entrance like someone has put a spell on you. There are two walls on either side, and moody light projections from the ceiling.

'Ruins,' I say. 'I didn't realise we were looking for ruins.' You examine each piece of stone carefully, but I shut my eyes and listen. I can hear people shouting. I can see red dust and smell the autumn air. I can hear the sound of swords falling and wheels turning.

❦

I can see the dome of the cathedral the other side of the wobbly bridge. The bridge is below me. People are walking across it and boats are heading under it. The sky is like a painting with a hole in it for God to see through. There's a map telling me where things are. I wonder where you are. I go over to the map to look, but you're not there either. An arrow points out the cathedral, the bridge, the train station. It's colour coded, making the bank of the Thames look flat and garish. The bridge is blood red and St Paul's is indigo. I want to see a picture of you, your shape, shaded orange, a number and an arrow, a paragraph on the legend below. This is where she is today, of all days, the day you want her, and there behind her, proud, and tall, round and dangerous, coloured luminous on the map is the Roman Amphitheatre.

If I could pinpoint you from here, then I could find you. I close my eyes and feel like I did when I used to pray for things when I was a kid in bed. I close my eyes, and when I open them again I want you to be there suddenly on the map, or waving at me from the real London below, not cartoon London, waving at me from the bridge, or the top of St Paul's, or one of the expensive riverside flats, or from the train going into Blackfriars, or from the red crane that's perched over a building site waiting for fish. Maybe God will write your name in the sky with an arrow.

'I can't find you,' I whisper to myself. 'Where are you?'

❦

British Library

From the second floor of the British Library I could see her standing next to a giant worm that was emerging from a stack of books, covered in words. I watched her walk up and down from the shop to the information desk. She looked at the leaflets twice. She bought a postcard and a pencil in the shop, then she got onto the escalator. It was her red hair that made me notice her. The good thing about the British Library is the capacity to watch people below you, milling about, reading, chatting. She looked as if her head were on fire. I imagined blue flames, and yellow ones, but there weren't any of those really: just orange, leaping up towards the ceiling. Her face was pale. She had freckles. I noticed that later when I followed her into the toilets. I didn't think about it at first. I watched her absentmindedly while I stirred my coffee. Her hair was like a beacon.

I thought something like this: Look at her hair. She's going into the shop. There she is again, by the leaflets, hair the colour of Mars. Then, a few minutes later, she came into the second floor café and bought some lemon cake, and sat down at the next table to mine. I'm not lying. That's exactly what she did. She took the postcard and the pencil out of her pocket and put them on her tray, just like that, next to her cake and her tea. I wondered who she would write to: someone in another country. Iceland, Mozambique, the Cayman Islands. Or maybe she would draw a picture. Perhaps she drew pictures on postcards for a living.

When I was sure she wasn't watching me, I looked more closely. The postcard showed the front of the library. She had a green dress on. She looked up and saw me staring, so she edged her seat away slightly – the way people do when they catch a person examining them – and ate her cake with a fork.

That was when I decided to follow her. I finished my coffee quickly. I gazed at the quotations on the wall until

I heard her chair scrape. I gave her a head start. She went into the Rare Books and Music Reading Room. As I entered, I saw her in a corner leaning over a desk. I sat down at a computer and pretended to search for books.

Green, I typed, *woman, dress, fire, hair, postcard.*

No search items have been found with your key words. Try again? I looked over at her. She had white gloves on – the kind the librarian gives you for examining old stuff – and was reading a small red book. I couldn't see what it was called.

Lemon cake, I typed, *fork, rare books, worm statue, pencil.*

No search items have been found with your key words. Try again? I found a piece of paper and a pencil on the desk and tried to form the words into a poem. It was half an hour later when she got up, leaving the book on the desk, and went out of the door. I was halfway through trying to fit *postcard, leaflets, escalator* into a stanza, but I couldn't spell escalator. I can now, because I've looked it up, but then I hesitated, and that's what I was doing when she went towards the door. *Esca, esco, ecsalator, escalater.* I left the poem behind on the desk unfinished and hurried after her. At first I thought she had gone, but just in time I saw her heading into the Ladies'. I went in behind her. As I pushed open the door, she turned to look at me. It was then that I noticed her freckles, and how fairy-like her face seemed. She locked eyes with me just for a second. They were green. That moment felt like a magic spell. All her stories exploded out of her in a thousand different directions.

A woman was changing a baby's nappy at the nappy station next to the sinks. She lifted the baby into the air. The red haired woman and I each went into a cubicle. I peed as fast as I could. After that I looked at my face in the mirror while I washed my hands: big brown eyes, droopy curly brown hair, saggy half moons of skin under my eyes. I had got onto examining my teeth for coffee stains when she came out, and I saw her reflection as she washed her hands behind me. I left the toilets and hid behind a pillar. She began to climb the winding stairs to the third floor.

I ran to the lift. It was slow, but I arrived in time to see her heading towards the courtyard garden. The courtyard garden is a semi-circle of benches with lavender and hanging leaves. I go there to sit and think sometimes. You can watch people walking around below; the cars and buses look like toys. I feel like a spy because they don't know I'm watching them. When I go there I'm a spy bird. I zoom over their heads. I hear their noise, like the seaside. The buses are like gulls. The traffic is like the sea dragging stones along the beach from up here.

The day I followed the woman with red hair, I went into the courtyard behind her. I felt like I was safe because this was my place. The place I came to watch. My trysting place. It began to spit with rain. The red brick library buildings hung about next to us like a mechanical cake. I felt cold straight away. There were people waiting for her. I felt deflated by them. They seemed too ordinary. I went back inside to get another coffee, this time from the vending machine with the small brown cups. 20p. It tasted of melted plastic. I watched them through the window. She shook hands with the people she had come to meet. One of the women - she had on a pink blouse - lent in and hugged her. I felt irrationally jealous. They sat together, the friends, two on the bench, three on the floor. The woman I had been following got out her sandwiches. But you only recently had lemon cake, I wanted to say, but I didn't. I couldn't. The pink-bloused woman got out a flask. The plastic mug steamed when she passed it round. Probably soup, I thought, she looks like a soup kind of person. These are the other things I thought: I wonder if she is cold. I wish I could sit out there with them. It must be good to be the kind of person who doesn't mind eating soup and sandwiches in the rain. I wonder what kind of soup it is.

The woman I had been following shared some of the soup. She drained the beaker and shook out the dregs behind her. She looked up. I was worried she would see me watching, so I went back to the lift and all the way back to the ground floor before I even let myself think about it.

I hung around downstairs by the escalator, kidding myself I wasn't waiting for her. After a while, I spotted her through the crowd. She went to get her coat from the locker room. I waited for her, then I followed her across the courtyard, past the coffee shop, up the road, past the hotel, towards Euston station. At Euston we got on a train to Manchester. I had to buy a ticket for the whole journey because I couldn't ask her where she was going.

The grey sky hung around the train like a friend who wouldn't leave. She changed at Crewe and got onto a smaller train. I took a chance and jumped on without buying another ticket. I was lucky; there was no inspector on the smaller train. When we got to her stop – I don't remember the name – she queued to get off, so I queued too. What if there is someone there to meet her? I thought. Another woman with red hair. This new woman might have hair in a long plait down her back, and say they had the same face, so I could see they were twins? What if they were wearing the same green dress? What if the woman I had been following pointed to her dress and her sister's dress, said something about being psychic, and they both laughed, and turned and noticed me there?

But there was no psychic identical twin with a plait, or if there was she didn't meet us at the station. I say 'us' because I had started to think that we were making the journey together. She walked across the car park towards a Vauxhall Cavalier. I knew it was the right car because she got out her keys and aimed them at the locks from a distance, making the lights flash. The day was getting late and the sky greyer than ever. I heard the train announcer's voice in the distance. I watched her. She was distracted. She patted her pockets. She took out the pencil and the postcard and readjusted the British Library paper bag around them carefully. I realised they must be a gift. I saw a blanket on the backseat of the car. I jumped in and lay underneath it before I could think about it.

We pulled out of the car park. She had trouble reversing out of the parking bay. It took several attempts. We went backwards and forwards and the engine spluttered. The blanket smelt of dog, which felt comforting at first, but then cloying. My nostrils felt clogged. I tried lifting the corner of the blanket so I could breathe. Thank god it was nearly dark. I saw her hand on the gear stick, her long fingers, her red nails. I had flattened myself against the seat. She stopped and pulled the handbrake on. From what I could tell the car was at an angle across the car park.

The twilight outside was misty and damp, and the headlights illuminated a bollard and a sign about parking fines. She took her jumper off and threw it on the backseat. I ducked back under the blanket just in time. The jumper landed on my head. Now I could smell dog and floral body spray. I waited, feeling hot and car sick, until the car began to edge slowly forwards; it stopped, and then the engine steadied to a low growl and we were on the road. I risked pushing the jumper off my head. In the dark I saw her tapping her fingers on the gear stick. Until that point I had been caught up with fear: tangled in it like a net. Now I was lying in the dark I felt overwhelmingly the sense of being in someone else's life: instead of being caught in a net, it felt as if I had been hit by a wave.

We stopped at a roundabout. I ducked back under the blanket. She put the radio on. A DJ, far too cheerful for the atmosphere in the car, chirped away like an annoying bird. I wondered where we were going. So many different possibilities: a secret space depot where she would change into a polyurethane suit and go through a gate to another dimension, a liaison point where a guy in a long coat would hold a gun to her head and bundle me roughly off the backseat and tie us together by the wrists, a National Park where she would do the nightshift as a park ranger, rescuing owls and stoats and moving dangerous branches, or was she on her way to meet the man or woman, men or women, she was dating, having an affair with, charging for sex? Was she the carer for an old woman with dementia who went wandering at night and had to be tracked down in a Vauxhall Cavalier? Or was she a night bus driver, and we were on our way to the bus depot, or a member of a coven, or a house breaker?

As I tried to calm myself with possibilities, we took a road off to the left, through some trees. I could see the silhouetted branches, the tops of them, like fingers, as I looked up through the passenger window. It was proper dark now. I risked propping myself up by one elbow. She was bobbing her head along to the radio. We went past a park, and houses with neat front gardens and hedges, then I could see, every so often, an abandoned bike or a scooter, lit up by streetlights or passing headlights. We stopped at another junction. Under the blanket again, I listened to the click-click click-click of the indicator, felt the pull of the engine, and its relief as she changed up the gears again. We had been going for about ten minutes. The car slowed. We turned a corner. A minute more and we came to a stop. I could tell we were under a streetlight by the pinpricks of light coming through the blanket. I got a sudden, stomach-lurching feeling of dread that she would reach behind for the jumper and pull the blanket away. I managed to stick out a hand and grab the jumper by the sleeve. When I looked quickly, she was doing her lipstick in the mirror. I hid again, hunkering down into against the seat as she turned. I felt her leaning back, feeling for the jumper. I pushed it towards her. She didn't notice me. She grabbed it and jumped out of the car. I felt the rush of cold air as the door opened, and heard new sounds from outside: muffled traffic, a pedestrian crossing. Then the door slammed.

I was still in the car. I sat up. She was already walking towards a house. It was mid-terrace, and small – the sort estate agents call a cottage. The front garden was long and thin. Lit up by the street light, it looked like a neat slice of green cake. Tall flowers bobbed at the edges: delphiniums, I thought, I wonder if they are delphiniums? By this time she was halfway along the path. I pressed my face to the car window. The glass felt cold. I realised I was shivering. The front door opened. I tried knocking on the window at that point, but no-one noticed. Warm yellow light held out its arms from inside, beckoning. The woman stopped. I watched as a moving picture played itself out in that doorway. Older woman in an apron, smiling; a medium-sized dog bouncing around her feet, a younger man with red hair, patting her on the shoulder, another man kissed her, older man shuffling in the background. I realised I was longing to be part of that picture. Longing, like a kid longs for Christmas presents. They probably hung around on that doorstep for a few seconds, but it carried on playing in my mind afterwards so time became irrelevant. Although I couldn't hear anything, I imagined:

'Come inside and get a cup of tea.'

'God, you look shattered. How was the journey? Train ride OK?'

'Tea would be lovely. Thanks. It was fine. Had to get the Manchester train.'

'That jumper is nice – have I seen that before?'

'I got you a little something. Let's go in and I'll show you.'

'I've made sandwiches because I didn't know when you were going to get here.' I felt hungry when I imagined sandwiches. A brief examination of the glove compartment revealed half a packet of Rolos, which I ate while I watched the house and imagined:

'Turn the heating up, it's freezing.'

'You got heating in that clapped out car of yours?'

'Come inside. Get warm.' And I imagined the TV in the background – I could see flickers of it behind the curtains, which were thin enough to let the light out.

Once the door closed, I could see shadows moving about behind them. I watched for a long while, growing colder, and gradually the shadows grew less frequent, and the TV stopped flickering, and after one final shadow crossing the room, the lights went out, and the house was left in darkness. I had the blanket. It seemed thin. I wrapped it around me and sniffed a corner, nostalgic for the possibility of the journey from the car park, wishing I had the dog on my lap to keep me warm and not simply the smell of dog. More than anything, I wanted the flickering TV and the yellow light and the tea. I thought of knocking on the front door, but it seemed impossible. Eventually I fell asleep under the blanket.

The next morning, someone who was probably her brother drove the car to the supermarket with giant headphones clamped to his ears. I jumped out while he was waiting in a queue in the car park and made a run for it. I think he saw me, but I don't think he knew I had jumped out of the car he was driving. I ran for the supermarket. I made it to the toilets. I had a wee and splashed my face. Then I got lost amongst the giant yellow signs advertising special offers and low prices, and ended up wandering amongst the tuna and other tinned fish, and up and down the coffee aisle, not knowing what to do next.

❦

Hospital

I fantasise about having everything done, changed, not only my face; arms, legs, stomach, then more specifically elbows, belly button, the outside of my left thigh. As I lie down flat on the trolley, my hair spread out around me, I can see myself from above, smiling. My hospital gown is pink. Ten minutes earlier, they injected the pre-med.

Everything seems happier, floatier, more whole. The nurse takes away the pillow and the sheet. Lying differently means I can stare at the square ceiling tiles, contemplate the mottled pattern on each, and the edging, how it comes away at the corners sometimes, the round electric lights – a uniform distance apart – and a yellow stain, the shape of a cartoon dog, lolloping across the ceiling. Beneath the tiles must be miles and miles of electric cable. I imagine the engineers and electricians on ladders, the ceiling half-finished, before there were patients.

Before there were patients there were miles of empty corridors, opening out onto empty theatres, wards, empty bays, not yet theatres, only spaces with no people. Empty rooms with no equipment; no one had died in the empty room then, now someone dies there every other week, with a new set of stone-faced relatives. I pretend to see the cable as I lie on the trolley. Blue and yellow and brown, thick stuff, not the kind you get inside a plug, running its own network around the hospital, like a set of tube tunnels for electricity.

We travel down the corridor, and now I think about what's inside the walls, insulation, cement, a souvenir left behind by a builder who wanted a stab at eternity, a handprint, a dropped Coke can no one could reach, so they sealed it in, a body laid to rest in the cavity, hidden cash from a robbery, a run-away hamster, making its living off bits of sealant oozing between the panels, hair and dust. I imagine the hospital in two-hundred-years-time. Demolished, or left to ruin, wind and rain in the corridor, dead leaves, trees growing in at broken windows, slamming doors, KEEP OUT and NOW WASH YOUR HANDS signs littering the floor, broken wheelchairs upended, pipes, toilet seats, yellowed and moulded paperwork spilling out of an upturned filing cabinet, an old computer monitor upturned and reused as a home for mice, who have chewed through the wiring, over-burdened sockets still full of plugs, the bones of a severed hand where the mortuary would have been, a metal cross on the floor of the Chapel of Rest, toxic dust in the pharmacy.

We pass a woman in a green overall pushing a trolley full of hospital library books. Why does the hospital library think everyone wants to read large print novels by Patricia Cornwell? Maybe they don't. Maybe those are the ones they're finding hard to give away. The thought is fleeting. It looks like a crow taking off from a branch inside my head. One minute it's there, then it's flown away. Or maybe it looks like a pair of crows mating on the top branch of the tree on a cold grey day in February. Or maybe it isn't a pair of crows mating after all, it is a black plastic bag caught in the tree, or a blue one in silhouette against the sun, tattered by the wind, and it can't take off because it's stuck, and will be stuck for a hundred years.

I think about when I was a child, diving in and out of the sea. I'm wearing a brown and orange swimming costume. The salt water goes up my nose. It is the most fun I have ever had, sinking under the waves, reappearing. I only feel frightened of the water later, as an adult, looking back on the memory. At the time, aged seven, it was a pure version of happiness, sea water in my eyes and long wet hair tatty about my face. That memory is stuck on a loop like the tatty plastic bag in the tree. Now it's gone.

Now I remember being five, and everyone at the party bringing me a colouring book. The carpet was yellow with brown swirls. What happened next? I'm ten, and my parents have bought me a Bugs Bunny lunch bag. I'm fifteen, and my mum has wrapped up a black and white bag with fake fur like a cow.

We go in through some double doors. The surgeon

talks to me about something, I don't know what, they do it to make sure you're anesthetised. When you stop talking, you're out. When you stop dreaming, you're out. His hand is hairy and the veins are pronounced. He has short fingernails. I notice this when he lowers the mask towards my face. It seems to hover there for a moment, larger than life, before it descends. He carries on talking to me, and asks me to count. I have forgotten how to count for a moment. Then I do it. I start at a hundred. I don't know why. The room seems to be full of light, light streaming through a window from somewhere. I don't know where.

The room must have windows in every wall, above the double doors, above the sinks and the cupboards, in the ceiling, although I know that isn't true because I have seen the ceiling tiles with the mottled pattern. They continue in this room too. The light must be coming from me, from my face. I wonder if he is secretly marking my body: arrow on my leg, star on my finger, CUT HERE on my arm, dotted line around my ankle, TEAR ALONG LINE CAREFULLY down my right hip, UNSCREW LID on my head or REJECT IF BUTTON DEPRESSES, PIERCE WITH STRAW on my foot. I'm drifting off, I can hear my voice faltering: one hundred and three, one hundred and four, one hundred and five. I can feel my eyelashes fluttering. I'm losing the squashing feeling of euphoria, now it feels like I've been bouncing on a bouncy castle but haven't landed. I'm still going up.

My face. Or more specifically my scar. The doctor is going to fix the scar on my face, skin graph, plastic blending, synthetic appraisal, melding aversion therapy, redecorating, replastering, reshaping. Tomorrow I will look in the mirror and I won't be me. Tomorrow I'll be someone else.

Nile Rivers

By the time Nile Rivers was nineteen, he had eyes that folded in on themselves when he thought about stuff, and opened up wide when he was surprised; messy hair, hard-working hands and arms, T-shirt and jeans. Nile was good-looking, sure. Slightly effeminate with a don't give a fuck but look at me anyway expression. It didn't seem like he worked on his appearance. He was natural looking. He had nice boots. He had a sexy way of smoking too. Women sometimes turned and watched when he crossed the road or leant out of the window of their car as he drove from the Lowcost to the wholesalers' with the order book.

But all the same, in nursery school he had got his heart out, put it on a plate, and given it to Pearl Leigh. He was embarrassed by how big his love was. As far as he could tell from the way the other boys talked, it wasn't normal. Nile only ever wanted one girl, and it made him feel as odd as a monk, but also calm. Once he had taken his heart out, and he felt it as a literal thing, imagined the stitches and the space, he couldn't feel anything stronger than a vague tightening of the chest for anyone else.

Pearl would one day be his wife, like milk goes in the fridge and the bread arrives in a van with a picture of a baguette on it, and she would be next to him every morning from that moment on, right? At least, that's how Nile thought it all panned out. That's how he explained it to himself every day. One day, one day, one day. One day it would all come OK. Turned out, though, that vague tightening of the chest he felt for other people, now he had given his heart away, he would probably have called it indigestion if someone had asked him, which they didn't, that tightening was a sign that there was something underneath trying its damnedest to break through. That something was a sense of him on his own without Pearl, without anyone.

Probably because of all that, Nile figured something wasn't quite right about Dave and Tommy walking around out in the daylight like normal people, like they thought they fitted somehow. They made Nile angry. The only place they fitted was getting the Cure for Homosexuality at the Pastor's Reform Project. Nile couldn't work out where his hatred came from, but he knew it was there and it made him uncomfortable. It wasn't right. It wasn't natural. He had no idea if God was real or as made up as Santa Claus, but all the same, God didn't want it that way. They shouldn't be allowed to walk along the same street as him. He felt it as a slight to him and Pearl, because Pearl was one of the Pastor's daughters. Him and Pearl were always meant to be together. Him and Pearl were natural. They were right. Always had been. They were the way God intended. He wanted Pearl so bad he hated anything that contradicted it, and Dave and Tommy were saying, just by existing in the world, they were saying things that are normal ain't necessarily so, and that put Nile on shaky ground.

Nile Rivers had started to grow apart from his father. He had looked up to Houston Rivers all his life but just now he experienced him a little like a bit of gristle he might leave on the side of his plate. He felt embarrassed that his father ran the Lowcost, even though he felt proud that he and Pearl would run the shop together. It didn't make any sense, but there it was.

Houston Rivers went along with things. People can't help who they fall in love with, his father said, when conversation turned to the Reform Project. When one of them came into the store with her collection for the salvation of the homosexuals, Houston refused to give any money. Last time he gave a tin of meatballs though, and that's what annoyed Nile the most. Thing was, they had to pray for everything they got at the Reform Project, so the Pastor had to send his family out to ask for food. Houston was so easy going. Why give the meatballs if you disagree with it? Why argue about the money, then give the meatballs? Nile wanted to be the kind of person who had opinions about things; unlike his father he wouldn't give meatballs when he disagreed.

Nile had dreams about knocking out the front of the store and putting up an ice cream stand. That was only the start of it. He would enhance the cold meat and cheese section too. Maybe get them fancy yoghurts. So Nile had started to form opinions and to disagree with his father. It's not possible for them to be in love with one another, he reasoned with the imaginary person in his head. He had never felt attracted to a man himself, unless you counted the football posters on his wall.

Nile liked to walk close behind Dave and Tommy. They held a curious fascination for him. He liked to whisper stuff he heard on TV, like *faggot* and *unnatural* and *queer*. He followed them early one morning when Dave had called into the Lowcost and his father had served him and, get this, Nile thought, telling the imaginary man in his head, get this, even *asked Dave about the weather,* as if he was some kind of normal person.

Nile slipped outside and saw Tommy waiting, and when Dave joined him, he followed them. Nothing overt. Nothing too violent. He was too scared of his father for that, too scared of what Pearl might think of him. But he walked close. He picked up a stone from the gutter and threw it. It hit Tommy in the back. Tommy turned. He looked worried. Nile remembered that look for a long time. When he thought about a person being worried, he saw those blue eyes. He couldn't help it. He didn't want to think about Tommy, but it happened anyway. Tommy turned: 'Hey,' he said. 'Watch what you're doing.'

'Queer,' Nile said, as quietly as possible. Dave turned too; Nile had to take a step back as he came closer.

'Watch your mouth,' Dave said.

'Go to hell, queer boy.' This was about Nile and Pearl being right and Dave and Tommy being wrong, wrong, wrong. That wasn't the only time Nile taunted Dave and Tommy. It became a regular habit. Nile knew the particular places they hung out. They went a certain way because Tommy worked at the garage, opposite the YMCA. Nile had it mapped out. At first he didn't deliberately try to remember the nuances of their days and the routes they took, but it stuck in his head, and then he found himself hanging out in certain cafés and on particular street corners, and he couldn't kid himself that he wasn't waiting for them.

He never did more than throw stones, or whisper, or walk too close behind them. He liked to think of himself as a warning: go on like this and no good's going to come of it. It felt strangely powerful to watch their reactions. Dave got angry. Tommy got worried, too worried, to Nile's mind. It was a game after all. Why did he act like the sky was about to fall down? A couple of times he asked him, still in a low whisper: *What are you afraid of? What are you afraid of?* but the worry on Tommy's face, a bit like grief, just got worse. It increased little by little every time.

What Nile didn't realise, because he wasn't able to look these things square in the face, was that low-level violence, everyday violence, is strong. Maybe not at first, but over time, it's strong, it's like a stream wearing away at rock, a weed pushing through concrete.

Falling

Fourteen. That's only 168 months or 5113 days. The savagery of the beating, the rough pull of his hands tied behind his back, it reminded him of the time he fell off his bike when he was five years old and he went rolling over and over and wouldn't stop because he was on a slope and he busted his teeth and broke his arm. His arm wasn't ever quite right after that and he figured it was probably broken again now.

It made him think of the time his mother bought a fridge and because of a dare with his brother he removed the shelves and climbed inside it, curled up like a foetus, and somehow the door closed. Perhaps it was his brother who did it, and he was stuck in there, suffocating. When his father opened the door he rolled out, in somersaults like he did at school on the gym mats, and his lips had gone blue. He felt dizzy. He felt that same dizziness now. His father hit him across the back of the legs with the belt of his trousers, while the trousers slanted across his backside, revealing his underwear, about to fall, until his father decided he had had enough and pulled his belt back on abruptly, like when the abuse stopped for days at a time.

It made him think of the time when he crossed the road aged eleven and the neighbour reversed his car right into him and he fell, and the neighbour stopped the car just in time and jumped out and waved his arms around and spoke really quickly, but he didn't remember what he said. It was like someone speaking under water. His mother said he was concussed and made him stir the dinner for hours, like that was the cure for concussion. It smelt meaty, fragrant and fruity.

He separated himself from the abuse, as if he had become two people. One version of him was in the body being beaten, the other floating high above, like a mini-god, god of the basement they had got him in, flying. That version of him was super-rational, could see every flake of paint and stain on the wall, smell the urine, hear the insects. That version of him couldn't move away because a thin but determined thread tied him to the other him, his body.

The roughness was like tumbling: the bike crash, the fridge, the neighbour's car, the meaty smell of the stew, and the whole time he could have been inside the washing machine in the window of the laundromat; the top loading one that juddered as the washing cycle kicked in. It was as if he were inside the washing machine in the laundromat window and the bike, fridge, car, the stew – like pictures – were all in there with him going round and round and round.

When they pulled him up the stairs, the stairs that went round and round and round, he could hear his heart beating so hard he figured that they all must be able to hear it. There were four of them. One of them had a phone and kept taking photos – he could hear the shutter sound effect. He had a tiny moment of superiority – they didn't know how to mute the phone. Ha. His heart was like an irregular drum. He was sweating too, like he did when he had flu and his mother wrapped him in blankets and told him to sweat it out.

The stairs went round and round, but it was the moment that they stopped that shocked him, the air hitting his face, or rather the air punching him in the face. Still, it felt like he was in that washing machine the whole time. They pulled him, making him stumble, wanting him to go faster, faster. Then suddenly they were in fresh air and even under the blindfold the change of light hurt his eyes. He could smell dust, heat, pollution, the breath of the man nearest to him and the coffee they had thrown over him that first day, still staining the front of his T-shirt.

Then he got to the sudden shocking moment when he was free, no-one touching him, not even the ground. No walls. No rough hands. No breath on his neck. Ordinarily it isn't possible to think very much in less than five seconds but the time he spent falling stretched like elastic. In fact, he probably thought of all of these things at once, like his brain was able to see an almost infinite pile of photographs in one go rather than sequentially. He got that mini-god brain again, the one that could fly – but now it was almost unhooked from his body – as tentative a connection as a balloon on a string held gently in his fist – but at the same time he was falling, falling, falling with his body. He was tied and untied at the same time.

Here are the things he thought about: his sister's wedding, his mother's hands, go-karts, fishing, his father's face, a football match, climbing over walls, a Sony Walkman, the ribbon-like sun. His head filled with the colours at his sister's wedding, green, purple, orange, the dancing and the music. He felt happy: a fleeting moment of happiness. His mother's hands: his small hand in hers. Her hand on his forehead. The last time she touched him. Her fingers brushed his cheek when they broke into his home and took him away. When he realised for the first time his hands were bigger than hers. When her hands started to look frail. Her hands on her daughter's face. Sad, gentle.

More things he thought about: the game his friends played together when they got broken wheels off the scrapheap and bits of wood to make go-karts. The thrill of the thing actually working after they spent weeks and weeks adding, amending, fixing, finding the rope to tie in a loop so his friend could pull him along, the rough rope burning his hands, unbending, the excitement of his friend pulling and running, getting faster and faster.

The time he went fishing with his father. The smell of the clothes his father wore, because he only ever wore them fishing - musty, damp, muddy. The dusty grey of the rock. The look on his father's face. The crease on the side of his cheek. The sound of traffic in the distance, perpetual but blurred, like he was rushing through the air. He remembered he was rushing through the air although it didn't feel like that, instead he felt cushioned by it.

At the same time, he thought of the football match outside his house that went on for what seemed like hours, the smell of the dust and the sheer joy he felt that day. He didn't name it as joy or call it anything else at the time. He felt like that football match would go on forever and ever; maybe part of him was still playing it now and would always be playing it. He could hear the shout of the other boys and the feel of the ball against his leg and the thud as it hit the wall they had as a goal and the group of kids that gathered to watch who were longing to join in. He was longing to join in now. Longing, longing, like he was falling, falling.

They had played in the early morning when the air was still cold and in the afternoon and evening because the air was so hot at noon it scorched his lungs, but in the late afternoon as the temperature began to fall, they came creeping back out of their houses again, shouting and gathering next to the ruined houses to find their goal again.

He thought about climbing up over the ruined wall, he and his friends daring each other to get higher and higher, the feel of the rough stone under his hands, the hot air in his lungs, the secret Sony Walkman his friend has stashed in a nook in the wall; a Sony Walkman that still worked. There is a craggy bit where two walls meet that used to be someone's kitchen where there is shelter and a bit of shade, where they feel safe. A broken picture still remains. They sit and listen to the Walkman and laugh. That tinny sound coming through the dusty headphones. He thinks of that, too, and the sun coming through the cracks in the brickwork, slants of sun like ribbons, like slides. He felt as though he was sliding one of those now, as if he were on a helter-skelter, or on an impossibly fast horse galloping, falling, or a super-long slide that goes on forever and ever.

All the things he won't ever do. He never was brave enough to sing to one of those songs on the dusty Sony Walkman and he wanted to sing; he wanted to sing at the top of his voice. He wanted to stand up on one of those walls and sing as loud as he could so heads stuck out of doorways, so his neighbour stopped his car and got out to stand and hear him sing. He wouldn't ever know what it was like to look into the eyes of his own child, to be bigger and stronger and older than a child, to hit him with a belt out of terror because he nearly died in a fridge, to take him out onto the rocks to catch fish, to see the creases growing along his cheek in the mirror day-by-day and to realise that his mirror image was becoming like his own father's mirror image, and he couldn't ever know what it was like to lose a parent. To him the thought of it was giddy, like going down those stairs they had pulled him up but in reverse, head over heels, like he was in an elevator that wouldn't stop falling, falling. He knew what it was like to see his mother and his father's face for the last time but – he realised, all at once with everything else – it was the wrong way round, he was supposed to see them take their last breath and still be alive, alive, alive.

Oddly, he felt more alive than he ever had before. He was in love with being alive. In less than five seconds he didn't have time to contemplate not being alive anymore. Death isn't something you experience, rather, you experience being alive right up to the moment that you die. He knew that now, although that particular bit of wisdom didn't have time to slot into place in the jigsaw of wisdom inside his head. He heard noise: shouting, the ground getting closer.

It isn't the fall that kills you. It's the sudden stop. His spine snapped near the top, severing the blood vessel that carried oxygen out of his heart and around his body. The thin thread that joined the two versions of him together snapped at the same time, as if that thread was attached to his body in that exact same place. Then they cut his throat.

The other him, the super-rational him, wasn't attached any more, and it carried on falling, falling, through the dust below his body, through the top soil, through mud and water - he felt himself like part of the water, air, water and empty space - through shingle and bones, and mouldering trash, old coins, lost treasures, fossilised teeth, and large stones and even crystals, and hard brown rock.

For about twenty miles he fell through the Earth, into hot rock that gradually softened like butter and got hotter and turned to magma and spat and seethed around him, hotter and hotter and he was still falling. This part of the fall felt like it lasted days and was orange. Then he fell through liquid, like falling through boiling syrup - this was white hot - then he fell through solid rock again. He was vaguely aware he was falling through the centre of the earth and that falling through the centre had an effect on him; it changed him. He had no longer resembled his previous self. He was the shape and colour of a white dart and still falling.

He went through the liquid syrup on the other side of the Earth's inner core, through the mantle, the soft butter-like rock, through the Earth's crust and the mud and dust and out into the air on the other side of the world. Through the Earth's atmosphere of nitrogen, oxygen, carbon dioxide, pollution, the blurred human noise and lights and smells and then he got too far away to see any of them anymore. Gradually the lights started fading, the air got thinner and colder.

He fell through thick, damp cloud until he floated above the clouds where the air felt volatile and unpredictable, as if a storm were coming, until suddenly he was in the stratosphere, and suddenly the storm threat had gone. The air was perfectly still. There was no weather, no water, like a desert in the sky, above him - although he didn't have a sense of above and below anymore - was dark blue, and he was falling towards it. He had no understanding of speed or direction, although he was falling upwards fast. It was as if he were hovering in a giant blue jelly.

Now he was frozen, at the furthest edge of the Earth's atmosphere. He could see giant shooting stars above him, then they passed him and fell to earth below him. He saw trails of blue-white ice crystals that glowed like paths leading him to different stories, different lifetimes. Suddenly he was at the beginning of space. Nitrogen and oxygen buzzed and played around him. Towards the North Pole he could see the solar winds creating the aurora borealis, which danced and blinked like the sound of an instrument in an orchestra or a murmuration of strange birds.

Gradually he was enveloped in darkness and the space between things got wider and wider, the stars brighter, and he fell out of the Earth's atmosphere. After three hundred miles he realised he was falling through space, falling, falling and still falling. Fourteen, only about five thousand days, not enough to sing in or to become a parent or to see himself grow old, but enough to begin falling. Enough to fall through everything until falling itself stopped, or rather, falling became everything.

Flash

You Are Not Special

In Clissold Park the trees look like they are praying, Pentecostal-style, raising their arms to heaven. The green and grey has a hint of white today: white grass and a frozen stream. His breath mists as he wanders next to the waterless paddling pool, then trots over to the dusted playground. He trots to try to warm up, but the cold air makes his chest feel like it could explode. He pushes open the orange gate and walks to the sandpit. He balances along a white log until a toddler fixes him with a hard stare. He thinks of his mother at the top of narrow stairs.

'You are not special,' she said, before she told him to leave.

He goes to look at the slide he used to play on, with hard ground at the bottom, and at the crazy red climbing frame where random children reach the top, muffled with coat, hat, scarf and gloves. He doesn't have any of that. He sticks his hands in his pockets. They look mummified against the frozen blue sky. There are slippery leaves on the toy pirate ship and hardly any pigeons today. He wanders towards the café and hears coffee spoons clinking and smells bacon sandwiches. He looks to see how much money he's got. His hands are so cold it hurts to take them out of his pocket. Not enough. He contemplates stealing something, but it's not easy here because the food is lined up in front of the staff. He would have to pretend to be someone else collecting an order, and he isn't in the mood today. He hears the sound of a brass band playing. Some couple are getting married. He stands and watches them go past. The guests are carrying balloons. He watches deer inside their houses for a while and then totters down the road, numb from the cold, people looking at him funny because he isn't wearing a coat. He notices: coloured vegetables contrasting with the grey pavement, a shoe shop, a record shop, post office, chemist, the number 73 bus, smell of curry, coffee, pollution, piss, beer, a scrappy backyard, an alleyway, bread, cake, cats, and, for sale on the street, books, records and toys. There are people having breakfast outside, mainly smokers. He passes the toy shop and the bus stop and goes into Abney Park Cemetery. He is met by brambles and angels, some armless or headless. On the graves the giant vases, or maybe they are trophies, are crumbling. He hesitates next to a shifted grave lid, dead bindweed twisting up from inside, like impossibly thin arms. He breathes in the earthy, overgrown garden smell, and looks up at the leafless trees, the evergreen trees, and the cold sky. All around him are: trodden grass pathways, overhanging branches, singing, dead flowers, hard to make out names, *in loving memory of,* moss and lichen, *safe in the arms of Jesus now,* cold stone, a lone bird singing, beer cans, a homeless man's sleeping bag, discarded, covered in ants, singing again. The light is fading. *You are not special* is buzzing in his ears like a ringtone that gets inside your head, that grasps hold of your brain and squeezes. He goes back to the sleeping bag and spends time examining it, shaking off the ants. He's going to need somewhere to sleep. He contemplates crawling into the sleeping bag here and simply lying on the ground, but realises it's going to get much colder. He finds a monument dedicated to *loving wife and mother always with us* but can't make out her name. The door has fallen in, ivy creeping around the walls; he thinks he might be able to squeeze inside, then he sees a dead rat decomposing in the corner and changes his mind. He stuffs the sleeping bag under his arm and walks further. Along the end of the path, in the fading light, he sees a mausoleum. He rubs his eyes. It looks like it's glowing. He tells himself it's the sunset. His foot catches on a bramble and he stumbles forward, a crumbling angel lands next to him, its head leaving its body and narrowly missing him. He stands again and makes his way towards the glowing mausoleum, sleeping bag in tow. He realises the singing has been there at the back of his mind ever since he found the main pathway through the gravestones. He gets closer. The singing gets louder. Now he knows the singing is coming from inside. It's almost dark now. The mausoleum is shining. He stumbles towards it and peers in. He sees damp stone walls covered in moss and ivy and a choir, lit by a floodlight, singing without music, their voices clouding the air.

The Christmas List

Emma made her Christmas list after Christmas. It wasn't a list of what she wanted, rather a list of what she'd received. Then she liked to hide it under her pillow and convince herself over a plate of pickled herring and savoury biscuits that she had wanted each item on the list.

Emma looked at herself in the bathroom mirror. 'Received', if she was being honest, was the wrong word. She had received them from herself, her other self, her shopping, sniffing, rummaging self, the self in her reflection. Emma haunted junk shops in December like a cold that won't leave. Portland Road had a bunch of them, blooming like odd shaped flowers, contents spilling out onto the street. She brought her finds back to her bedsit and wrapped them carefully in much-used wrapping paper.

Emma's rooms weren't much. She lived above a sewing shop. She could hear the machines going in the night. Her mum used to say they were up to no good. She could still see her Mum's outline in the armchair if she scrunched up her eyes. The bathroom was untiled. Unfinished, she said in her head, but it never would be finished. In slow, curly handwriting she wrote:

Vase, fish-shaped
Stuffed komodo dragon
One-way ticket to Liverpool from 1982
Small Japanese cushion
Old piano music
Clock with words instead of numbers (broken)
Salt and pepper shakers (1940s)
Black and white photo, wedding day, promenade at Brighton (1930s)

Emma looked at the photo. That couple had probably been happy the whole of their lives, had kids, grand-kids, great-grandkids, and were buried together in a tiny churchyard at the end of a winding path, hidden from view by tall hawthorn hedgerows, or he got drunk and hit her, and when she finally got up the courage to leave he drowned himself, or the man took a boat out to sea one day and everyone thought he was drowned but he had started a new life selling cloth in a market in Honfleur, and when he left her the woman was incredibly poor, but she met someone who, but Emma had fallen asleep with the pen in her hand.

Fragments Found in a Tunnel

These fragments were found next to human remains in the ruins of a tunnel in Greenwich.

If you are reading this, it means that you've been unlucky enough to arrive in London, even unluckier to wind up in the tunnel, and that you are stuck. Let me provide some orientation. In the days before London became a prison, people used the tunnel to travel backwards and forwards between the Isle of Dogs and Greenwich. Down in the lift one side. Up the other. All day long the lift attendants sat and listened to their radios, one in the Greenwich lift, one in the Dogs lift, crosswords in hand. They had no sun, no view of the weather, if anything they got hello, goodbye, thank you, cheers, mate, bruv, over and over, and they got to watch the ghostly black and white shapes on the TV screens above them. Some people say the lift attendants are still here. Sometimes I hear their radios crackling. Sometimes I see them checking the tunnel with their torches.

If you're new to London, you'll need to know this. Runners have created a new kind of service, part messaging service, part protection racket. Messages can be sent from any tube station to any other. A Waterloo to Embankment - a short dash under the river - is fairly easy. Anything else, they take their life in their hands. The runners risk the sudden unexpected power surges from independent generators, rats, and gangs who sometimes set up tollbooths in hidden chambers between stations. Runners spend all day and night in the tunnels. Like Roman Gladiators, there are champions and fast losers, and a slain champion can easily be replaced. They are dangerous story-spreaders. It is runners who circulate the new London legends.

Within a few years the legend of the lift attendants had spread from Victoria to Putney to Barnet and Piccadilly Circus and out to Morden on the disused Northern Line. The foot tunnel had been sealed for years. The solar panels that began to appear all over London appeared here first, and they keep the lifts working. The story-spreaders say it was the lift operators that did it.

The London legends say that the lift attendants were simply forgotten about, and that one tells the truth, and the other always lies. The story goes that when everyone else was evacuated they didn't get to hear about it. It was as if they were moles who lived all the time in the shaft between above and below, that they didn't even realise they were dead. It's more likely that, for some reason, they chose to stay. There were a few who disobeyed the enforcement orders, mostly those who loved someone classed a criminal, those with somewhere to hide, anyway. Others were dragged from their homes in the night raids that went on for months before the vast concrete mixers arrived. But the story-spreaders call the undead lift operators the Oracles. They say that the only way you can consult an Oracle is if you get thrown into London, then you have to seriously offend someone, enough to get brought here.

The anti-chamber is a concealed escape route. The London legends disagree about how and why the tunnel anti-chamber was constructed. Perhaps to give a tiny glimpse of hope. Or simply a traitor's gate, a way of bringing the undesirables here to die. It is clear that the tunnel is a prison within a prison, that if you end up in the tunnel, someone above does not care for you.

❦

In the lifts the walls are chocolate brown. There is a bench and a plaque with facts about the tunnel – how many tiles, when it was opened. Of course, no-one walks the tunnel anymore for getting from one place to the other. Once you get up to the surface, the lift doors open onto silver metal panelling and no way out. No door, only smooth shiny walls. Study them with your hands and feel the curve; you're inside a small and perfect dome. Above you, through toughened plastic, you can see the sun playing on the solar panels; the panels are everywhere, powering the whole of London, but there's no way to walk out into it from here. The same the other end: down to the tunnel, up to a perfect dome, shiny walls, plastic, sun, and no way out.

❦

If you are left here without diving equipment or knowledge of the anti-chamber, you go mad (hence the London slang 'tunnel madness'). Not a brief irrational anger or mental instability but gnawing, mind-blanking madness, like a rat burrowing, biting, that won't let go. The white tiles, the dripping, the damp smell, the round walls, the pipes lining the roof, the rust patches, the echoing of the radio from the lift – and the rat starts.

❦

The Law of the Wall: Surround the capital with a wall of concrete, just inside the M25, move in all the petty criminals, the car breakers, persistent vandals, fine evaders, as well as the molesters, serial murderers (crimes of passion were exempted because some MP had killed his wife) and armed robbers. The usual system is to be woken at 5am by armed police breaking down your door, drugged, taken by helicopter to the roof of what used to be University College Hospital. It doesn't land, of course, so people who experienced landing on concrete have dragged deteriorating mattresses up there to soften the fall. The only other way in is by parachute, since the concrete wall was built. There were stories about a gate, but that is probably a myth. Some have attempted to swim out, only to be met by a great concrete dam just before the Thames Barrier. Newcomers arrive in groups, with food for the first few days in packs. Sometimes newcomers get separated from the rest of the group, especially if they come by parachute, which is bad news for them if they land in gang territory near St Paul's or the Globe or St Katharine's dock, which are strongholds.

❦

Once you've been sent to London, there is no way out. Occasionally, anthropologists hover, like giant birds, over Tower Hamlets, Walthamstow and Crystal Palace, in helicopters, studying community formation. You've probably seen them. Some prisoners claim they are post-doctoral anthropologists from the University of Oxford sent to London on purpose. Others don't believe them. If you are a prisoner, you can live in Buckingham Palace, the Houses of Parliament, or the best wharfside apartment you can find, but you can't leave, and nothing from the old days works. The electricity, phone lines, water supply, gas, petrol supplies were all cut off months before the wall was constructed, just after the last resident left. All of the water, the shanty electricity, fuel and communication lines were organised by prisoners after the wall went up. Those who were already in London prisons woke one day to find the doors unlocked and all the prison staff gone. Apparently, they walked down Pentonville road towards Kings Cross in huddles, led by the bravest, and found deserted shops, empty roads, dark traffic lights, and no noise, only birds calling out to each other.

❦

I have spoken with the Oracles and have discovered how to get to the anti-chamber. Start at the lift with the tarnished panelling. There's no other way to tell them apart. Measure seventy-two tiles on the left, then fifteen up from the floor. Underneath are the controls to the anti-chamber. Press the red button once, and then slide back the drain cover to your left. That's the anti-chamber. Inside you'll find a pothole big enough to squeeze through. If you have no diving equipment you'll have to hold your breath. You have a fifty-fifty chance of making it.

Taffeta

I close my eyes and see a shop window full of colour.

'You were found wandering around Covent Garden. Can you tell us what your name is?' I remember a shop window, bright colours, toys, a hot air balloon, teddy bears, crêpe paper, coloured string, golden balls, with my face arranged in miniature in each one. Taffeta. Fake cotton wool snow. Taffeta. Why do I remember that word? It is an odd word, a colourful tinsely word. The word is something to hold onto. Taffeta. It sounds in my head like a drum, so I use that because I cannnot think of another word to use. The shop window, sweets, soap, candles, *Alice in Wonderland* on the front of a book. Taffeta, sounds like a drum, like a bell.

'What's your name?'

'Taffeta. Taffeta. Like a drum.'

'What did she say?'

'What's your name?'

'Taffeta.' The doctor writes Taffeta Leikadrum on the forms by my bed. The nurses call me Taffi, so now that's my name.

I remember a band near the shop: a brass band playing a loud tune. I turned from the shop window and there they were behind me. A crowd of people started to gather. I didn't know where I was going. I felt lost, but I had no destination, no reason to go anywhere. Next to my bed is a cabinet. I steady myself on it and stand up, get out of bed and look out of the window.

I can't remember where I came from, but I can count things. I can count the things outside the window, close my eyes and say it back to myself: cars, trees, road, rain. I count the things on my bedside cabinet: water jug, cup, flannel, lamp, book. There is a clock in the hall. I can see it through my open door. It is white. Everything is white, apart from the green walls in my room. When they found me, the band shone like pennies. The faces shone. The French horn shone. I felt like a stone on the beach, a stone that can be turned over. There's something underneath. I feel like a stone with something underneath. I don't know what is underneath. Cars, trees, road, rain, book, lamp, jug, clock, flannel.

There is a picture on the wall. I close my eyes and try to remember what is in the picture. If I can remember what's in the picture, I might get my memory back. I count on one hand: pink blanket, white chair, in it, a wide brimmed hat, cut flowers, branches, the wall of a house, blossoms on paving stones. I look and realise that I remembered everything in the picture but the wrong way round: a pink chair, a white blanket, blossoms on a fallen branch, a hat on paving stones, flowers climbing the wall of a house in the distance. I have remembered everything apart from: there is a swooping bird in the sky above the house. I imagine that it is a kestrel, that it has seen a field mouse, that it is hovering above the field mouse ready to dive.

I close my eyes and try to remember everything in my room, one after the other. Room: green pale walls, white tiled floors, bed, white floral duvet, untidy pillows, bedside table, jug, cup, flannel, lamp, door open, clock. Outside the window: rain, cars, trees. In the picture: pink branches, a white hat, flowers in a young woman's hair, a ruined wall, a blanket fallen to the floor. I have forgotten the kestrel again.

When I look back at the picture the kestrel is no longer there. He has flown away, I think. I go closer to the picture. Push my face up against it so that all I can see is the picture. No kestrel, no dormouse, no field mouse, no vole or stoat or baby rabbit, no swooping and diving. I look out of the window to see if I can find the kestrel. Not there either. Not in the trees or near the cars or flying through the rain.

When the nurse comes to see me, I am sitting on the edge of my bed counting all the things in the world: pink things, blankets, chairs, kestrels, dormice. By the time I get to branches I lose count and have to start again. Houses, flowers, tiles, clocks. I tell the nurse I am worried in case I cannot remember everything. She says it is normal after a shock. I go into the dining room and eat too hot cabbage and steak and kidney pie with a fork. There are other people there. Have they also forgotten who they are? I lift my plate up to my chin and tried to spoon the gravy into my mouth using my fork, and keep my eyes on the TV. The gravy scolds my tongue.

There is an overhead screen stuck on the wall above us like a crane in a nest with one huge eye. Then the news comes on. I see a picture of pieces of a boat washed up on a beach and a body on the beach. The words: people trafficking, illegal immigrants, all on board must have died, Police looking for the ringleaders. I remember: storm, waves, wind, beach, vomiting on the pavement in the dark, train station, shivering, train, sleep.

I hear what happened next as if it were happening to someone else. I hear my plate clatter to the floor. I hear my fork hit the table. I feel the gravy burn my legs. I put my hands over my ears and then over my face to try to stop myself leaking out of my own mouth. Arms lift me under the armpits and someone injects something in my arm. I feel tired.

'Taffi,' I hear the nurse say, once I am back on the bed. When she thinks I am asleep and leaves, I whisper: 'Walls, floor, bed, duvet, pillows, bedside table, jug, cup, flannel, lamp, door, clock, rain, car, trees.'

Part Two

The Marmalade Factory

Wednesday was marmalade day at the Glasshouse. When I was a kid, I used to sit on a white cupboard with my feet dangling, and watch people moving around me, and wished hard that I knew where I was from because a kid at school said 'Where are you from?' and I didn't know the answer. A couple of times I had to move my legs because the cupboard where I sat contained the dry ingredients; mostly spices and sugar hiding in the brown interior. They seemed secretive and reluctant. When I was really small, I thought of them as treasures. I liked to reach inside and feel the rough wood under my fingers. I touched the special ingredients: maple syrup from Canada, banana rum from the Polynesians, sultanas from California, brown perfumed rice from Kashmir. Once I got older, I sat silently and watched, lifting my legs high in the air when Manda waved her hand or Irene bent her knees. I was allowed to sit there because I was Mary Arnold's daughter (and she was famous).

'Suki Sweetooth sucks sauce on a spoon.' Manda and

Irene loved tongue twisters. I got my nickname from a tongue twister, because I sometimes sucked a marmalade covered spoon when I was small. My real name is Camellia, like the flower.

In the marmalade factory, the people were dressed in white, so it felt like we were inside a mysterious clinic or laboratory. I didn't have a white shirt and trouser suit, a white apron, or white cap with a net. I felt like a sudden heap of clothes, the ones people leave outside charity shops on the street, a sudden reminder that clothes could be a different colour. I was multi-coloured: brown face and hands and feet, mixed paint fingers, eyes, and hair, plus as many different coloured clothes as I could find.

I watched Manda stirring with her stick, the only one she would use; she was superstitious. Orange, green, gold, pink, blue and purple. Those were the colours that made me. I remembered it like a recipe, like the Marmalade recipe we all knew off by heart: *1lb sugar for every 1lb oranges plus ½ lb orange rind, water and mixed spices*. I wondered if my mother had made up the Japanese woman and her part-Native American husband, to fill in the gaps in her head where parents should have been, or if she really knew who they were.

There I was, multi-coloured on top of the cupboard, lifting my legs when I had to, watching. Manda and Irene had been joined by other staff now. The whole of the ground floor was given over to the industry of it: stoves, cupboards, freezers for the ice cream, fridges for cream, mixers, mixing stations, fruit-chopping boards, crates, jars, boxes of sugar.

If you paid, you could go through the shop and stand on a special viewing platform outside the factory area. A recording of someone famous giving facts and figures about marmalade played while the visitors stood and watched. I had to wear a hat in case anyone saw me. Today I had a green one, with yellow flaps over the ears, because it was

November and I was cold. People started at me sometimes and pointed.

'That's her daughter,' they mouthed, and took pictures, so I had to pretend not to notice. Then they moved on to the shop to buy recipe books, prints of my mother's paintings, postcards, knick-knacks, and lavender pot-pourri.

Some days we made jam too, while half the floor worked on packing and jarring. Wednesdays was only marmalade. On Wednesdays there were three main colours: green, from the plants outside that crowded the glass like children wanting to get in, bright orange from the stacks of fruit that were piled up at intervals along the walls, molten brown from the mixture itself, with occasional gem-like glimpses of peel.

I am named Camellia after the factory's original name: Camellia House. In old pictures it is long and thin with a glass roof and circular domed centre - a Victorian greenhouse - and I liked to imagine rows and rows of plants sprouting where the fruit boxes were stacked: Purple Petals, Snapshanks, Lily Lemons, Venus Fly Traps, Mini Cacti. The watering cans smelt of wet metal while big leaves curled around the insides of the domed roof. Nobody calls the Glasshouse by its old name. Even my mother calls it the Glasshouse. I'm not called Camellia either. People used to try out bits of my name: Cam, Leah, Mel, Cammie, but never all of it. Now those who know me call me Suki after the tongue twister. A lot of people call me 'Mary Arnold's Daughter' with capital letters. (My mother is famous, so it figures.)

When she started the factory, my mother had everything that wasn't glass painted white. She said it was cleaner. Even the weather vane on the domed roof was white. She made it. She gave it the same logo as the plastic bags in the shop: an orange with two leaves and an arrow going through it, like a cupid love heart, with *Marmalade Factory* in curling letters around it. We had drawn pictures of factories at school. Mine was tall and dark with a big chimney and small windows. When we first moved to the Glasshouse, the idea of a factory made of glass and painted white with a weather vane on top seemed like the oddest thing ever. When kids at school asked me where I got my name, just to see what expression they would pull I said I was named after a factory.

'Were you born in it?' one girl asked me. We were working on project about the Industrial Revolution and poor children who got their fingers trapped in the machinery.

'Was I born in the Glasshouse?' I asked my mother. She smiled the way she did when she had reached the point with her painting where she knew what it was going to look like. When she could see the whole, that was when she had reached the top point of her climb, and she could roll all the way down the other side.

'No,' she said. She wasn't looking at a painting when she said it. She was looking straight at me.

'That was where...' she said, then she broke off and laughed like she usually did. I filled in the gap, like I usually did.

'That was where you fell in love?' I suggested.

'Right,' she said.

'It was where my mother fell in love with my father,' I said to the girl at school.

'Was that where they did it?'

'Did what?' I said.

'You know. Did it.'

'Oh,' I said. I thought about the cold slate and the thick green plants that crowded the windows.

'Is that why you're a funny colour because your Dad did your Mum in the jam factory?' she said and she giggled at the thought of it, like I was another variety of marmalade-related food. No, I thought. 'Yes,' I said out loud, because my mother had told me that the best way to deal with bullies was to agree with them. I looked at my brown hands. 'Yes, that's why I'm this colour.'

We went on a visit to a factory as part of our school project. The inside was huge. I stood in the middle and looked up towards the ceiling, and felt as if I could have been lost in outer space. The man who showed us round said it used to be a button factory, but now it was a museum, and he gave us a quiz sheet. I wondered why they needed all that space to make buttons. Maybe once they had to make a huge button that filled the factory right up to the ceiling. I drew it on my quiz sheet, but the teacher told me off. After the factory visit, I changed my story and said I was named after a flower, and it sounded much better.

'No you weren't. You were named after the place where your mum and dad did it,' said the girl next to me. I pulled her plait hard and made her scream, and she never said it again, and when we went swimming I put an earwig in her hair.

When I was small, around the same time I liked to taste sultanas from the wooden cupboard in the factory, I asked my mother why I was brown, and she said, matter of fact, mixing her brush in the green pond-like water and contemplating her painting: 'Mix two complementary colours and you get brown.'

'Which colours?' I said to my mother as I roamed around her painting studio picking up old brushes and jars, staring out of the yawning window that she had had extended because natural light is so important. She put her brush to the canvas again and began to fill in the blue, the water.

'Put that down,' she said. I was playing with a sheep skull. She had brought it back from the beach for a still life.

'Which ones?' I said.

'Orange, which is why you like oranges so much. Dark green, the colour of the leaves. Blue, from the flowers in the garden with the big leaves outside the glasshouse, because that's where you were...' She stopped and reworked her sentence: 'That's where your father and I....' We both stared at the splash of blue across her painting.

'Where you fell in love?' I tried again because I wanted a romantic story. I felt if I insisted on it enough times, her memory would warp, and then stick like that. I liked the story about my mother and father to end in them falling in love and me being born.

'Yes,' she said. 'Big leaves. You can still see them. We fell in love.' Then she stopped talking, and that meant I had to supply the words. I marched up and down, examining the sheep's skull where the eyes would have been, the smell of painting around all three of us: mother, daughter and skull.

'You were in the glasshouse looking at the blue flowers and the big leaves when you turned around and fell in love.' In my stories, falling in love was always sudden, and happened after turning around. I imagined that one day I would turn around, and there, on the spot, I would know what it felt like. My mother said love was fizzy, an Alka Seltzer in water.

'What other colours?' I said, handing the story back suddenly.

'Oh. Gold, and pink and green and silvery grey,' she said. She filled in petals, pink ones, with flecks of white for light.

'Always look for the light and the spaces,' my mother said. She liked to give me random advice about painting.

'What colours were *you* made of?' I said, although I knew the answers. I put the skull down and stood with my arms out at an angle. Kind of you-can-hug-me-if-you-want-but-I-don't-care-if-you-don't half raised arms. She wasn't going to hug me, not with her paint brush full of pink paint, but I stood like that when I wanted her to tell me things, palms towards her, fingers spread. She thought about it.

'I wasn't made from colours. I was made from ingredients. Like a cake. It's different.'

'Oh,' I said. I only really knew about marmalade and different flavoured jams. Although I had seen Manda make Marmalade Cake for the café, cakes felt mysterious to me.

'My mother, *your* Grandmother,' she said. 'Well, I used to imagine she was from Japan.' Because this was another conversation we had had before, I knew what to say: 'Didn't you know for sure?'

'No.'

'Wouldn't anyone tell you?'

'No. So I imagined it. I imagined the Kimono,' she said, daubing the petals.

'And her mother was from Kerala,' I said. 'So she was half Japanese and half Indian?'

'Right,' my mother said. 'But she had a grandfather from the Sudan and a great-grandmother from Peckham. Ingredients, see? Currants, flour, sugar, ginger, eggs, water, butter.' She continued to brighten up the flowers. 'My father, well, *his* mother was part Native American, part Presbyterian Scottish…' She paused to add some yellow to the background.

'And part Kentucky good time girl?' I offered, but she didn't stop to confirm or deny it.

'And his *grandfather*,' she said, suggesting sunlight with a shaft of blue-white, 'was a British Colonialist, poor as dirt, a prospector really.'

'A what?' I said.

'Panned for gold.' She gazed at the table where her still life was arranged, working out the position of the pebbles.

'I was left at a children's home, you know.' She decided on a grey-blue for the first stone. She told me she was left at a children's home whenever she wanted to change the subject or whenever something good happened, to the point that, years later, whenever something good happened to me, I would say it under my breath. When she sold a painting, when she had enough money to buy the Glasshouse, when it was finally restored and she opened the factory and the shop, when the Tate proposed a major retrospective, all of those times, she rubbed my hair so she messed it up and got flecks of paint in my fringe and said 'Not bad for someone who was left at a children's home', then I would get extra pudding for tea, even if I was full and couldn't eat it: jam tart and custard, apple pie with marmalade ice-cream, cherry tart with orange sauce, meringue with cream and layers of mandarin. And because she also read me fairy tales at the same time some of these good things were happening, because of the gingerbread houses and the old woman who lived in a shoe, I imagined a children's home made of candy canes, with hundreds of children leaning out of the window, and a big blue paddling pool for some reason, probably because I wanted one and couldn't have one. It was only when the children's home had closed down and she took me to visit that I stopped thinking of a house with candy walls whenever she talked about it.

When we went to visit, the doors were swinging to and fro, and leaves were blowing around inside because of the broken windows. It smelt like a hospital. There was a long dormitory on the top floor that still had the small beds in it. My mother was a celebrated artist by the time we climbed the stairs and looked at the green paint peeling from the walls. I imagined a lady in a Kimono and a man with long black plaits dropping her off at the front door. In my imagination it was stormy, a nurse took my mother and wrapped her in a blanket. I looked at the front door step. My mother must have watched it every day and wondered, like she watched me every day and wondered, as if I were a map or a compass or a genie or the North

Star.

I was good at art because of my mother. It made the other children hate me. Once the art teacher told us about colours. At the end of the lesson, he said:

'Now, has anyone got any questions about colours?' One girl put her hand in the air.

'Why is Suki Arnold brown?' The art teacher went serious and looked from me to the other faces turned towards him.

'Suki Arnold is mixed race,' he said in a slow careful voice. It was the first time I had heard anyone say it. I was amazed at the way the words hummed above my head as if I wasn't even there.

❦

Now I am an adult, if anyone says Camellia, it makes me jump, as if they have used the name of a dead sister who I knew once and loved, or like a ghost has just brushed my shoulder. Lovers, thinking that Suki is my real name, try to shorten it to Suk, which makes me think of soup, so I don't like it. I told my latest lover about the tongue twister nickname. I whispered it to her when she was about to do it to me. I had given her a jar of marmalade sauce and she had the spoon poised, and it had reminded me.

'Suki Sweetooth sucks sauce on a spoon,' I whispered. She laughed, turned the spoon upside down and dripped sauce onto my nipple.

'It's a nickname,' I said. 'Suki.' She put the spoon back in the jar. I liked what she did with the marmalade sauce. I made her do it again. I made her eat me like ice cream and she made me melt away to nothing.

'What's your real name?' she said.

'Suki,' I said, because that name was as real as any other.

'Before that,' she said, tipping the spoon again.

'Camellia.' She sat up and smiled at me, like the new knowledge had made her see me differently. I was alarmed.

'Don't stop,' I said.

'Really?' she said. 'That's so posh. Camellia. I never knew you was posh. I thought your real name was Suzi or something like that.'

'I'm Mary Arnold's daughter. Of course I'm posh.' She looked at me as if she were seeing me for the first time. I grabbed her by the waist and pulled her on top of me so we were like a marmalade sandwich.

'Paddington could keep us under his hat,' I said, and she laughed.

'You're silly,' she said. 'Camellia.' She tried it out. Then she said it one syllable at a time. 'Ca-me-lli-a.'

'Sh,' I said, and I kissed her to make her shut up about it. Afterwards I took her to the Glasshouse to show her the place I was named after, and I told her about the plants and my mum and dad. The floor was still. The workers had gone. We wandered between the cupboards and the workstations, looking.

Philosophy For Beginners

I am in Norwich, in the Waffle House, sitting in the place I always sit in, imagining all the waffles I've ever eaten one on top of another. Imagine if they were all here now. If I ordered all of them, mushroom and cheese, ham and salad, ratatouille, plain waffle with butter, multiplied by the ten years I have been coming here. I would look like Scooby Doo or Shaggy making impossible sandwiches when the monster is chasing them. This is the place I used to come when things happened. (I would order waffle, chocolate mouse and cream. I almost couldn't eat it. I wanted to eat every mouthful. I wanted to dive into it, swim in it, drown in it.) I don't like the mirror next to the table. I can see myself as I eat. I can see the way my mouth turns down. The people around me speak in flat voices, like they are lazy, like they are yawning at the ends of their sentences. This is where I am when I read the story about the tree. It is the most beautiful thing I have ever read. I read it on a postcard, in a newspaper, a magazine, on the back of a cereal packet, in a recipe book, on a shopping list, on a bookmark, in a letter. I read it on a packet of seeds, on a menu, a bus timetable, a leaflet about the time the swimming pool opens, a prospectus, a poster, a price list, on the back of my hand. Then I walk along the road making up this story.

I was studying Greek Philosophy one summer when the woman I was seeing bought two vibrators, shaped like toy cars, one blue and one red. They were made out of soft jelly material, like jelly babies, and had white wires attached to them, so I looked like I was hooked up to a lie detector. When I was in class, I had to screw up my eyes tight to understand the words the tutor said, which sounded just above my head in a haze, like a summer haze when you look out of a car window and the road wobbles. I caught words and phrases when they dripped down from the ceiling. If I screwed up my eyes tight, I heard more. But those small square cars kept coming back into my head, and the pants she made me wear to keep the cars in the right place. My class was on a Wednesday afternoon. I had nothing else to do all week, but read and have sex with her on top of the covers because it was too hot otherwise. Sometimes I put my hand up to ask questions when I didn't understand something. The tutor always paused sadly after every question and gazed out of the window. I wondered whether she was thinking about the wonders of the world or the meaning of life because that's what philosophy tutors think about, probably. I did my hair specially for my class, in plaits, and I wore a hat and my *Queer Get Used To It* T-Shirt, so I looked cute and studious for my new lover when I got home, so that I could let her take off my hat, unravel me, and feed me avocado or asparagus or anything beginning with a, like anchovies or almonds.

I go out of the Waffle House and walk past the car park and the Futon Shop and Oxfam and the place I used to get off the bus when I was younger and Tesco Metro. I walk past the market, the City Hall clock tower chimes twelve as I go, sounding with my footsteps, every fourth step. I walk past the interesting street names: Lower Goat Lane, Dove Street, Colegate, Red Lion Street. It is sunny. It isn't supposed to be sunny here. I don't remember the last time it was sunny here. I walk up past the place where the man plays the didgeridoo and where the ice cream seller stands, the one I like to imagine sells any-flavour ice cream, like in the *The Magic Far Away Tree*. Elephant and sausage flavour, for instance, and if you ask for something for a joke, just to see if you'll get it, you have to stay behind in the magical land at the top of the tree and eat it until it's all gone. So don't ask for elephant flavour. You don't want to taste elephant ice cream. Imagine what it would be like to lick your tongue across the grey folds, across those eyelids, along the trunk and the tusk. You don't want to smell the breath and the mud. Or taste it inside you when the ice cream has gone, always taste it, the leaves and branches growing in your belly. I go past the ice cream man without buying an any-flavour ice cream because I am still full of all the waffles I have ever eaten, could ever eat, like Scooby, and I remember the thing about the tree and make up this story like I'm writing it down, but I'm not.

Once I was teaching a philosophy class. It was a hot summer. The students wore shorts, and shirts tied in knots, and sometimes peaked caps and sunglasses. It was Classical Philosophy For Beginners. I didn't want to teach it. I wanted to lie on the grass and smell how fresh it was. I wanted to kick my shoes off so hard that they flew into the air and hit someone. I felt disconnected from my words, like my body was lying on the grass and kicking its shoes and only my voice taught Aristotle's *Poetics* and set homework on Plato. I have a big garden. As I walk along the path, it feels like the plants are going to climb over my head and plait their fingers above me. As I walk along the path, I think about the story I want to tell, and whether it is this one or another one. I think about the philosophy class I taught last summer when it was so hot we could hardly move, when I fell in love with someone I couldn't have. I watched her through the classroom window. Outside there was grass, and beyond that a river where brown geese and swans played. On the grass, people came to eat food, or drink lemonade, or to lie in the sun. When I first saw her she lay on her back in an orange T-shirt and red shorts. Her hair was shoulder length and yellow as a lemon. Some days she ate a sandwich and read a book. Some days she lay propped up on her elbows, gazing at the river. Once the hot weather broke, it rained so hard it was painful to walk in it. From the classroom I could see the rain crashing into the river like hundreds of pebbles being thrown by a god. On the days when it rained, she didn't come.

'Did Aristotle live in a cave?' one of the students said, the one who had a T-shirt that said *Queer* tied under her breasts, so that I could only see the tops of the letters, so that it could have said Queen or Quorn, but I knew what it said because I had seen it before. On the back it said *get used to it,* in small letters, like an eye test. She was an optician's chart. I had to screw up my eyes to read it. She wore a white hat to every class so that I never saw her face properly. She had straw-coloured hair in plaits at the side of her head and a ring in her nose. I don't know what her name was. I don't remember any of their names. I remember looking out of the window on the last day of the rain, imagining the shape of my love by the river, and the impossibility of it, now the grass was churned up into mud. Then, suddenly, I saw her walking by the river in the rain with a blue raincoat and blue boots. The actuality of her made me feel like the top of my head had opened.

The optician's T-shirt girl asked about caves, just as I was watching the rain splash on my love's face.

As soon as the philosophy teacher has thought about the rain and the queer T-shirt and the cave, I go up past Nat West and the British Heart Foundation Charity Shop. I go past the place, which is closed down now, where the people were rude, but where you could get different types of cake and sit outside and have cakes made especially for you if you wanted to. I get to where you can walk down to the cathedral, or the pancake parlour, or Prince of Wales Road, past the Prince of India, past the Post Office. I imagine hundreds of princes lining the way, with blue and green flags. I think about how hot it is in the story I am making up. So hot the days melt like ice melts on a beach.

I remember it was hot last August. I was sleeping with a woman who had taken the summer off to study Philosophy. She was so sleepy on those hot days. She told me she wanted to lie in a boat on the river and listen to the water. From her classroom it was only a few minutes walk to where the boats were. People sat around on the grass all day. She spent the rest of her time reading, usually at home on the sofa, for all her talk about boats. I was busy. I worked in a café in the centre of the city. I wore an apron and took orders from tourists who filled up the seats with their arms and legs and necks and children. In the evening, I taught the philosophy student about orgasms. She had had them before, just not one after another, or at the same time as each other, which is what I showed her. How to layer them. How to wait. How to feel like a well full of swirling shape-shifting water. Clear and cold like that. I worked from 7 until 6, then I went to Sainsbury's and bought asparagus or lemon and chicken, depending on the letter of the alphabet we were on, and went home to cook for her, even though on everyday but Wednesday she lay in the house or in the garden with her books around her, and could have cooked a banquet for us every night with all the time she had.

❦

After my lover has fed me broad beans, raspberries, French bread, brie (she says she is feeding me bs today, although I say that raspberries don't count, and it should have been blackberries or blueberries) I lie on my stomach while she strokes my back and I think about Aristotle. I try to remember what the sad looking philosophy tutor said as she gazed out of the window and into the rainy day. Was she thinking about the meaninglessness of everything? We had the end of class exam soon and I was trying to remember what I had learnt. Aristotle argued with Plato, I remembered that. And Plato argued with Socrates, who drank poison. Who was it who argued with Aristotle? I screwed up my eyes. I couldn't think of it. I imagined them at a special training camp for philosophers on the side of the mountain, where they went to argue. It made me smile. My lover thought I was smiling because of the way her hand moved across my back tracing my curves. I did smile because of that. Was it the same training camp that Hercules went to, and where Apollo learnt to shoot? My Queer T-shirt lay screwed up at the end of the bed. My lover said I was brave to come out in my Philosophy class, and kissed me where my backbone ended. Euripides, was that it? Or did he argue with Hercules? I didn't realise then that the most important thing I learnt that summer was about orgasms, and not about philosophy at all. Tragedy, I thought, plot, then character. *Spectacle is the last thing on the list,* the tutor said with a sigh, looking out of the window. I wonder if she meant that spectacle is the least important, or if she meant there are seven (or however many there were, I screw up my eyes, but I can't remember), seven things that are important about tragedy. Plot, character, spectacle, but what were the others? I had forgotten. I thought about the vibrating jelly cars, turned onto my back again, and made her climb on top of me.

I could make a spectacle for you. Don't think I can't because I can, I can, I can. I could have been a juggler, green and white, with skittles or fire. I would do it just for you. I've written the beginning too many times, and I can't find the middle or the end. It's not like Aristotle said at all. There isn't a middle and an end, only a beginning. Aristotle was wrong. Once I came round to your house when you were in the garden. You were sitting on the bench that looks green and frail like it might collapse or leave a green mark on my legs. Now we are standing by the tree. I think you want me to read the thing about the tree. You seem excited about it. I read it. I read it again. It is an unlikely moment, standing next to a tree. I am not trying hard. I arrive on my bike or walking. I can't remember. And you are in the garden. You stand up and go over to the tree. Aristotle said begin at the beginning, middle in the middle, end at the end. It is a small tree, not very old. I am worried about poison in our flat because of the ants, and now it is like I am poisoned with it and I can't do anything. I can't stop it, and then there were ants in the garden of the new house, and for a minute I hated them, got the bleach and poured it over where they crawled. They had a burning acid drowning death. I had poisoned myself, poured bleach over myself. I was sorry straight away, but I couldn't stop the bleach from seeping. Then there you were next to the tree looking at the ants crawling up the bark and over the leaves of your tree. I wanted to say the thing that made it all right. The thing that afterwards you would remember. Instead you told me about it and what other people had said, and I thought secretly about my own ants and the bleach and the poison. I lie down on the grass in your garden and spread out my arms. Now I have ants running all over me, over my feet, toes, shins, knees, thighs, between my legs, stomach, back, breasts, arms, hands, nails, shoulders, neck, head, face, nose, eyes, ears, hair. I have ants all over me like that.

I arrive on my bike. It is a sunny afternoon. I don't know what I want even though you ask me. You are next to the tree touching the leaves. I can't remember what I said or what you said. You said something about apples and ants. Maybe I'll tell a story about it instead, where two friends meet next to an apple tree, and one day the apple tree will be tall and strong. It will have a beginning. It will middle in the middle, screw down into itself like mud does, like belly buttons. I was thinking this story in my head, but now I have written it down.

Here's a beginning: Once there was a woman who rode into the city on her bike. I feel like I'm in a room where a thousand light bulbs are exploding. I think about it in Asda, Tesco's, Sainsbury's, Waitrose, Iceland, Marks and Spencer's, when I take a can off the shelf and put it in my basket: beans, juice, carrots, spaghetti, ice cream, sweet corn, chocolate. In your garden there are giant leaves. I have to push past them to get in. There is the bench that looks like it's made of upside down tortoise feet, the one that I am frightened to sit on in case it breaks. You timed me once with your watch with arms the colour of clay and it hurt so much it felt like the watch hands were digging into my fists where my knuckles are.

There's a bit of the story missing. It has gaps as delicious as the vanilla ice cream you can get from the any-flavour ice cream seller on London Street. I go back to the Waffle House, so I'm back at the beginning of the story again. I look at myself in the mirror. The middle and the end stretch out in front of me in the mirror in different directions. That's where I read the story about the tree, and it's the most beautiful thing I have ever read. It shines like a glass of water with the light on it. I read it on an aeroplane, in a car, balanced on the handlebars of my bike, on the back of my friend's scooter, in a helicopter, in a truck, on the bus, on a National Express Coach, on a train, on a horse. I read it in a diary, on a laptop, on the internet, in a note on a scrap of paper, on a post-it, written in graffiti, in a cartoon strip, in a poem, on the wall of a pub, on the back of a toilet door, in a guide to safer sex and it's the most beautiful thing I have ever read.

García Márquez and me

Including García Márquez and me, there were six of us.

'This is Derby everyone,' someone called. I clambered into the van and pulled the dog in after me. We sat like prisoners lined up inside. One of them was called Obadiah. He had dreadlocks. He said to call him Obi, like I was pronouncing just the first two letters. It sounded like Obi-Wan Kenobi out of Star Wars. He had a girlfriend called Noah with woolly black hair extensions. I forget the other names. The dog couldn't sit still. I wrapped my arm round him.

'S'okay, Garçon,' I whispered, but I was nervous myself. I imagined Obi had a light sabre and a monk's cape to keep myself calm.

'Have you been on many of these?' I asked. Obi shrugged.

'We keep it up till they stop, right?' The van juddered to a halt and Noah opened the door. Obi's torch confronted me. He grinned.

'You alright?'

'Yeah. Where are we?' I asked.

'You'll see.' It was cold. I made out fields and a few low buildings. The others jumped out behind us. Noah got a screwdriver and worked on the few streetlights so they blinked out. We climbed onto a walkway with only the torch to guide us. It lead us round a car park. García Márquez came with us, but Obi made me tie him to the gate once we got clear of the car park. We went hand in hand in a human chain along a path to the back of the farm. The darkness was as thick as stew. Obi was at the front. He pocketed his torch when we got near the farm buildings. A house perched on the side of the hill above the farm. The lights were on, but we were hidden behind some low buildings. The ploughing machine looked like a monster, it was so still and silent. It glowed because the moon had just come out from behind a cloud. I smelt hay, manure and sweat. The moon went back behind the clouds and we were cloaked in darkness again. Obi held up a hand.

'OK. Come on.' We emerged into an open space. I saw the silhouette of a huge building, like an airport hangar but low on the ground, with a silver roof and a high fence around it. We hid behind a tree with sweeping branches that touched the ground.

'Only one of five,' Noah told me in a whisper. We saw someone walk round the building checking the locks. We waited until the figure headed back towards the farm. He made for the same path we had been on a few seconds before. He stopped as if he had heard something. A dog barked in the distance. García Márquez probably. I wished I had left him in the van. The figure moved away. We stayed back while Obi took out his pliers and ran towards the building. He broke a hole in the fence and got a foothold on the outside wall. He moved up a drainpipe and hoisted himself onto the roof. He rooted around in the backpack and unfurled a banner daubed with black paint.

It said: *Vivisection must stop now*. He was like Spiderman. He hung from one end of the roof and reached inside the gap at the top of the metal doors with the pliers.

I heard scratching from inside the building as we entered. The smell hit me: urine and dog food. I blinked at the light. The lamps made the air hum. I saw rows of cages and hundreds and hundreds of animals. The smell got stronger. I went over to the nearest one. It was brown with deeper brown eyes. It snarled and ran up and down its cage as outside the rain started. I hadn't ever seen so many animals at once.

'What do we do now?' I said.

'We open the cages,' Obi said simply.

'What are they?' I asked.

'Mink,' Noah answered.

'Fur, medicine, soap, electrocution, meat what difference does it make?' Obi said. 'We're setting them free.'

'But won't they die, out there?' I said. I looked out into the field behind us and back at the mink.

'They'll die if we leave them in here,' Obi said. 'At least we're giving them a chance.' He reached into a cage and lifted one of the animals by the scruff of the neck. It was terrified. It looked like a stoat but with a shaggy brown coat. It snarled and tried to bite him, so Obi put the animal down. It didn't know what to do at first. It ran over to the wall and stood in the shadows. Then it darted out of the doors into the night. I saw its face light up and the sleet glancing off its fur before it ran out into the darkness.

'What are you waiting for? D'you want to get caught? We could get five years for this.' Obi ran to the side of the building and began undoing the cages. The others followed him, opening cages as fast as he did. The growing swarm of mink climbed over each other, fighting each other, snapping and bleeding.

'Come on,' Obi said. 'Prove yourself.' I joined in. The mink continued to swarm. Suddenly, the animals began to dart forward out into the night. Someone laughed. I laughed too. Obi held up his hand. He'd heard something. A shot in the darkness. The whine of a dog and police sirens.

'Time to go,' he said. We scrabbled across the field in the dark and the mud. The sirens got louder. Obi knew another way out of the farm: through a ditch and over a wall and another field and through a narrow gap in a hedge. We crept back out onto the path on our hands and knees. I heard cars crunching across stony ground in the distance. Obi went on ahead. After a couple of minutes, he ran back towards us. His face looked white.

'Derby, come with me,' was all he said before he turned and sprinted back the way he came. I followed. I sensed the others behind me. I heard shouting from back near the mink shed. When we got to the place where I had left García Márquez, I found the dog on the ground, moaning to himself in a high-pitched whine. I felt tears running down my face, but otherwise I went numb. Obi had taken off his coat. I knelt down and wrapped it around him.

'Garçon,' I said. Torches bobbed across the field, and the shouts got nearer, but I had forgotten about being caught. Obi lifted the dog into my arms.

'They shot him,' was all I could say. I felt arms around me one on each side. Another shout.

'We're gonna have to run,' Obi said. 'Now.'

'Come on,' Obi said urgently. 'Gotta start the van.' I cradled García Márquez in Obi's coat while Noah tried to make me run faster. Obi jumped into the van and started the engine. I heard police sirens again. I climbed into the back with the others. Obi put his foot down and we headed off into the darkness. The dog's head rested on my lap. The sirens and shouting died away. García Márquez yelped quietly to himself. I put my face next to his ear and whispered to him.

'I'm sorry. I'm sorry Garçon. I'm sorry.' He looked up at

me. His eyes were red. I mean his pupils were actually red. Five minutes passed until we realised we weren't being followed. Obi drove into the rain, taking random turns, waiting for someone to say something.

'We need to find a vet,' Noah said at last. I stayed quiet. Voices buzzed around the van like a swarm of wasps.

'We can't stop. We'll get caught.'

'He's gonna die.'

'They'll be circulating our pictures already.'

'He's gonna die.'

'Pictures? No one saw us did they? Who saw us?'

'We're all going to prison for this Obi.'

'Pictures of known sympathisers.'

'He needs a vet.'

'We'll get caught.'

'I don't care. We have to get to a vet.' The rain was banging hard on the car. I saw lightening in the distance.

'It's OK. It's OK,' Noah said. 'We'll think of something. Just calm down, OK?' The dog moaned again. I could see the blood on the coat. His eyes rolled back into his head. I felt suddenly cold.

'OK,' Obi said. 'We find a vet. Derby takes him in. He's not known to the police. Yet.' I had to force myself to stay still. I wanted to open the door and run.

'Won't they be looking for someone with an injured lurcher?' someone said.

'Don't care. Get to a vet. I'll take him in,' I said.

'Listen. Just take him in,' Obi said. 'Ask them to look after him then get out as soon as you can. Leave him there. They'll look after him.'

'They won't just let him die will they?' I said.

'If it's a vet's, they care about animals, right Derby?' Obi sounded like he was trying to convince himself.

'OK. OK. That sounds like a plan,' Noah said. She was already jabbing at her phone.

'Yeah. Hello. I need the address of a vet that does emergencies. Yeah. Thank you. Thank you.'

García Márquez was breathing heavily and his eyes were closed. Still numb, I took the coat in my arms and went across the gravel car park to the animal hospital, while Obi hid the van under a tree. A nurse in green scrubs answered the door. He didn't look at me, just at the bundle I was carrying. He took him from my arms. The door closed behind me with a bang. I was in a hallway leading to a waiting room that smelt of dog biscuits and fur. I had a patch of blood on my jeans from carrying García Márquez. A receptionist helped the nurse carry the injured dog into a side room. Then the receptionist returned alone and looked at me like I was a piece of shit.

'I need a name,' she said.

'He's called García Márquez, OK?' I said.

'No. I need *your* name.' We eyeballed each other for a few seconds. She reached for the phone. Before she could dial, the nurse came out of the side room.

'I'll deal with this,' he said. 'Go and wash up.' The receptionist had blood on her dress from the dog.

'Stay there,' she told me, before she disappeared.

'How did that happen to him?' the nurse asked. His eyes were kind, but worried.

'Dunno. Is he gonna be OK?'

'Too early to tell,' he said. A disembodied voice – the vet presumably – called for assistance. As he went back into the side room, he jerked his head towards the door, telling me to leave because the receptionist was back. She went straight to the counter and reached for the phone again. I backed away. A moment later, I was sprinting across the gravel towards the car.

'Drive,' I shouted. Obi started the engine as we jumped in.

'They know about it,' I said. 'Saw it in their faces.'

'Is he OK?' Obi said.

'Not sure,' I said. 'They took him into a room, and then…'

'It's gonna be fine.' Obi drove us down winding side streets to avoid the main roads. We got lost twice and drove for an hour before we realised we were going round in circles. Finally, we found the right road. Obi stared wide-eyed out into the night. When I woke up, Noah was shaking me. The radio was on.

'We turned it on to hear the news,' she said.

'A break-in at a mink farm has resulted in the local area being overrun with mink. A spokesperson from an animal welfare group said that the mink are not used to the UK environment and will probably die of exposure. These animals should not be approached. Please keep doors and windows closed, as they may attack your pets. A receptionist at an animal hospital has identified a suspected member of the gang who freed the mink. He was seeking medical attention for a dog injured during the botched protest at the warehouse, but escaped before she could call the police. The dog has since died.' It felt like forever passed before anyone said anything.

'Botched protest. Shit,' Obi murmured to himself. The van sunk into muddy silence. The air in the van got heavy. I rested my head against the window. García Márquez was dead.

The House

She was going to the House to burn the body of her friend. Before she left, the woman with the green eyes reached into her bag for an omen. Bones and Death and the Tree of Fingers. The black bag was like night time inside, and like the night time, it was full of shapes and spirits. The spirit of the moon, she thought, thinking of the night creatures, voles maybe, badgers, owls with big yellow eyes swooping, inside the bag it was like that. She picked out the three stones as if she were playing scrabble and wanting to make words. She put them down one at a time on the table in front of her. The omen wasn't good. The Finger Tree meant danger, the Death stone meant a new beginning, and Bones meant that something would affect her deeply, or to the core, as if she were an apple and she carried around pips inside her, which were waiting to take root in her stomach, and would do if she ever ate enough soil.

On the day of the burning, before the fire was started, Rachel sat at the brown wooden desk in the library, which had marks etched into it from scratching with a pen on thin paper. If she put her palm on the desk, she could feel the indentations for the words she had made. She looked up from the book she was reading to help her forget about the body waiting to be burnt and gazed through the window. She looked out into the garden to where the white gate was, and the leaves - green and red and heart-shaped, spiky even - climbed up the gate and over it. Beyond the end of the garden she could see the thin line of grey, which meant the sea was there in the distance. The land was flat, but the sea was a while away from here, especially when she followed the winding paths with the hawthorn hedges, which she couldn't see over. When she stood still, she could imagine the bushes and the thorns closing in over her head, and if she stayed longer, lacing themselves into two locked hands. Rachel thought about the woman with green eyes who would come to light the fire. She had shiny green eyes, almost like glass. Rachel thought that her eyes were like two drops of the sea, scooped into the palm and left to drip from the hand onto the woman's face. They were like drops of seawater. Water containing monsters, because the woman looked as though she had seen things before, and that new things wouldn't surprise her or frighten her. Rachel wondered whether there was anything at all that would frighten the woman; perhaps there was one thing that scared her, nothing else. If only I could find out what it is, she thought, the thing that frightens her. Then she saw the woman come through the white gate, and she knew that it was nearly time. She left the book of adventures on the desk and went to get ready.

Benny was the oldest member of the House. She had white hair around her face, which looked like feathers. Her face had become as lumpy as an old mattress, and now that she hardly ever left her chair Benny was also as soft and as uncomfortable. Although the woman with the green eyes brought her stones with her, Benny had her own set, inside a wooden box, which she kept on the mantelpiece, and which she took out and shone with the corner of a scarf or the edge of her dress, and lined up in front of her. Rachel knew them off by heart, like a promise, because she had seen Benny set them out carefully, like dolls, night after night, and although she wasn't supposed to remember, she did. Bright red with grey marble flecks just under the surface, with three marks like someone counting to three quickly. One was green, but not shiny, pastel-coloured like a crayon, with a star in a circle. One was light brown. It had no markings, and although the top surface had been polished, the underside was still partly rough and randomly smoothed by sea water and sand, and Rachel liked to imagine it at the bottom of the sea, being thrown about by currents. There was a small white stone and a flat dark brown one, like the moon and the night, Rachel thought. The white stone had a mouth carved on it, and the dark brown one, an eye. Another was yellow with a curvy cross etched onto it, and the final stone was purple and was quite round, the same size as a sprout, and with the same cabbage leaf-like indentations on the surface. Sometimes Rachel thought it was like a planet with countries marked out on it.

When Rachel had first arrived at the House she had been frightened of Benny, or rather, she was frightened of the music that she played. When Rachel first arrived, she picked up the paperweight in Benny's room, and felt frightened of being trapped like the yellow and white flower in the glass, but the music that she heard Benny playing frightened her more than anything, more than small spaces or the yellow flower. Benny's room was on the ground floor of the House, because she was too old to climb the stairs. After her first lesson in forgetting, Rachel came along the ground floor corridor past Benny's room.

The music made her run quickly towards the door to the stairs. She ran through into the corridor. She couldn't find the light switch, so she went up in the dark, all the time thinking that there were fingers a few inches away from her, waiting to close around her face. Although she could no longer really hear it, the feeling the music gave her followed her along the landing and into her room, and so did the fingers, until she had turned on the lamp and had got into bed with her pillow over her ears.

When Rachel first arrived at the House, she went straight up to her room and she thought that she would never get used to all the things that were kept there, but now she couldn't imagine being without them. The objects stood in for memories, and helped her to forget the things in her head. Rachel's room was on the left side of the building at the top of a winding stairway. It was painted dark bluey-green, which made it feel smaller than it was. It would have taken a Stranger a week to remove each object out of the room, to wonder at each one, and then take them outside of the House into the gardens. Once all the things from Rachel's room were lined up outside the House, then the Stranger could look at them one at a time, in detail: chipped paint, dyed feathers, dark wood, green fabric. The wooden parrot hat stand. The paperweight with the perfect yellow and white flower inside it. A book of photos of the moon, a green chair covered in tapestry, musty books about Greek adventurers, candles in candle holders, pots, one with dried oregano inside, one with 'mustard' in grey letters printed on it. A jar of earth with a miniature garden. A scrap box full of recipes and, another with fabric pieces. A crate of old dolls. Scarves and three hats, a fountain pen in a stand, a comfortable old armchair, so old it was haunted by hundreds of stains and spills and hundreds of people who had fallen asleep in it. Buttons in a jar, too, and a rubber plant with large flat leaves in the corner. None of these things was hers. They all belonged to the House.

'Objects just are,' Benny told her. There was Rachel's bed next to the window, and a space on top of it for Rachel to lie down, and next to it for her to stand up. There were clothes discarded on the end of the bed and on the haunted armchair, mostly versions of the hooded tracksuit tops all the members of the House wore.

It seemed like a long time ago that she had arrived, but she couldn't remember how long ago it was. The House was a healing place, that was one thing she knew, and two, a peaceful place. They grew herbs and vegetables, and they sat in the sun in garden chairs. She had been there a year at least, she thought, because it was autumn when she came and it was autumn again now. Calendars and clocks weren't allowed at the House, and the members never mentioned the time. Now is important, one of the members would say, if she talked about yesterday. Writing was allowed, so was cooking and flowers. Most things apart from talking about the past were allowed. There were some things that were the same every day. They washed their hands in bowls of water next to them at breakfast, and ate lemon and cream, then bread, then more fruit of some kind. They kept their hoods up outside. The food was always good, and there were books, and the sound the sea was brought in on the wind sometimes. They could go out when they wanted to. There was nothing to stop you leaving by the white gate, following the winding path, and going on and on until the House was far behind, and starting somewhere else. One or two had done it. They had no car. All money had to be given in for the good of the House. But one or two had stolen money, or had walked the miles to the main road and hitched, and it didn't matter because they were yesterday, and that was gone, and it was the only way for a member to leave after all. No-one made you stay. Rachel walked the roads around the House often, after she had finished her jobs for the day. It was her job to write letters asking for donations to the House, and other letters about business, like selling honey and vegetables at a new market. She wrote letters at the desk in the library on thin pieces of paper, until her words became etched on the desk, one line of words over another.

Now that Rachel had been in the House for a while, she had got to know Benny and her music, which sounded like a woman crying. She often took her tea and biscuits, and went to sit with her in the long room downstairs.

When the woman came to do the stones, Benny liked to narrow her eyes and fix her with a stare as she waited for the reading. Then Rachel would have to pick up the tea tray and leave the room, even though she wanted to stay and watch the woman with the green eyes. Afterwards, Rachel was sometimes allowed back in to stand and look out of the window at least, and Benny would rise up straight in her chair, play with her feathered hair and smile. Then the woman with the green eyes would pick up her black bag and go out into the garden without saying anything else, and Rachel would watch her cross the grass with big strides.

On the day of the burning, Rachel was sitting at the desk in the library writing letters, but she had stopped to look at the stories in her favourite book. It was an illustrated copy of the adventures of Odysseus. The story of the Cyclops, the giant with one eye, had a picture of a green giant and a flaming torch. The drawings were hand-painted, and Benny had told her that the book was very valuable. She had seen the woman with the green eyes arrive and she knew she would have to go outside to the fire soon. The words of the book stopped her thinking about the flames of the fire, which already leapt about in her head.

Rachel picked up the paperweight from the edge of the desk. She had brought it with her from her room to stop her letters flying around in the draft from the library window. She held it above the words of the book and looked through it. The letters turned big and upside down, like it was a word crystal ball. She imagined that the paper wasn't there, and that she was looking into magic glass at the end of her stories, but they ran away from her like streams. The yellow flower in the paperweight could have been a spider, when she turned it on its side, with eight fragile legs and a white eye. When she held the paperweight just above her own words written in blue ink across the page, it magnified them until they looked like the tracks of a strange blue sea creature, or like electricity, and not like words at all. Or maybe the paperweight was like a large glass eye. A giant's eye watching her. Spinning it made the giant giddy. *Nobody is killing me*. Spin it and it makes the magnified words spin too. When it stops, tip the giant eye this way and that and you can sometimes make out the words. She lifted the paperweight. The words became the right size again. *Nobody is killing me,* the words said. Spin the word crystal ball around, and it will pick up a word or two and spit them back up to the surface. Green, sent, understand.

The woman with green eyes came to make bread every Tuesday. She did flowers too. She brought in bunches and laid them out on the table naked, without a vase, with the stems pointing towards the door. Then she would sieve flour and weigh the bowl in her hands. She made dough, which made the whole House smell of yeast. Rachel stood in the hall from where she could see a slice of the kitchen through the half closed door. Every Tuesday, she watched the woman kneading and stretching. As soon as Rachel heard the taps run, she knew that the woman would emerge with red wet hands to chop the stems of the flowers to the right height for the vases, and then she would retreat silently.

Once, in mid-autumn, just after Rachel had first arrived,

the woman came to make a bonfire, after she had swept up the apple flavoured leaves and the twigs in the garden. The flames were blue and orange and lit up the woman's face, but she didn't smile. She looked sad, like she was remembering things. Rachel watched her then and thought that her face looked beautiful in the firelight, but she went back to her room without speaking to her.

Members couldn't talk to Strangers, unless it was business talk about apples for the market, or selling herbs from the garden. A Stranger was someone from outside, who had memories that they had not forgotten. The woman who made the bread and did the flowers and the stones was a Stranger. The House paid her to help in the garden, too, and she took vegetables and herbs to the nearest town to sell for them.

If you leave the House you can't come back again, because you are past. The Stranger who made the bread was the only member who had left and had been allowed back into the House. She was allowed back because of her talent with the stones. But she wasn't a member anymore. She found it difficult to forget things. She was a Stranger now, and no one was supposed to talk to her about anything other than business. Only the one or two who had been at the House the longest spoke to her more than that. Like Benny, who couldn't remember her past before the House. She refused to remember, and now the past had actually left her.

'The past is a different place from now,' she said, when Rachel asked her where she came from before, and she smiled to herself. Then Benny put on her music, and Rachel wasn't frightened of it anymore. She had been at the House too long for that. She let the music into her head and closed her eyes.

Rachel told Benny that she thought the woman who read the stones was beautiful.

'She is, yes,' said Benny, stirring the tea that Rachel had

brought for her.

'She reads other things too,' Benny said when Rachel asked her about the stones. 'Bodies.'

'Dead bodies?' said Rachel. 'I know.'

'Live ones too,' said Benny, and she smiled.

When a member died, it was the woman who read Benny's stones who lit the fire, and then stood back while the members held hands in a circle with their hoods up and waited. A day later, when the bones that were left were cold, she read the head, naked of flesh, and told the members that their friend had been reincarnated to a place of peace or war or into a tree, or perhaps she said that the spirit waited at the House, unable to leave; Rachel had forgotten which. A tree should be planted where the ashes are, the woman said. And someone said that because the woman wasn't a member she shouldn't be allowed to talk about trees, but Benny told them all to listen to her, and the tree was planted. Later a member saw a dead face at the end of a corridor, and they gathered again, and covered their heads, and sent the spirit on with a broom and sprinkled water.

'She reads bodies. Live ones,' Benny told Rachel as they listened to the sad music.

'What about mine?' said Rachel.

'Come down to the library tonight. I'll arrange it,' said Benny, and she chuckled to herself.

It was the first time Rachel had spoken directly to the woman with the green eyes.

'Take off your top,' said the woman, like a doctor would have said in the time before the House. She took off her hooded top, and stood in the middle of the library, with the moon shining brightly through the window at her. She reached out the hands she used to break branches and arrange flowers and knead bread. She picked up Rachel's arm, and saw the scars crisscrossed over it in patterns, and here and there burn marks, too. The woman touched her arm and looked into Rachel's eyes. Rachel tried not to think about the knife she had used, because it was gone, like a leaf from an autumn ago. Or the blood that was bright and proved that she was still alive. In the House, she could remember doing it once - or was it twice? - although she was supposed to forget. The time she remembered, there had been no cigarettes, so she used a match from the kitchen. The flame was pretty. If she had done it more than once while she had been in the House, then she had forgotten it, she told herself. Now the pen she used on the paper, which was thin like skin and rested only on the wooden desk, was like a knife or a flame - the way the words got into the wood.

The woman ran her fingers over Rachel's arms and then her neck and face. Then she made her put her hood back on and sit down. The woman offered her the bag of stones. Rachel took three of them, like Benny had told her to do. She lay them out in front of her. She felt the knife-feeling come back in her stomach as she did so, even though it was past. Then she felt warm and safe, knowing that the scars were under her sleeves.

'Close your eyes,' said the woman. 'Put your hand above the stones. Now move them into a shape.' Rachel felt the stones under her hand - the rough parts and the smooth parts. Her hand was like the sea, she thought. She moved the stones into an upside down triangle slowly, one at a time, rubbing each one in her palm as she did so.

'Open your eyes.' The woman looked at the stones in the moonlit library and stayed silent.

'Tell me,' said Rachel. The woman got out a notebook instead, and drew the triangle of stones quickly, then she wrote in spidery writing underneath each one.

'Tell me,' Rachel said again, but the woman refused.

'Go to bed now,' she said.

The next day Benny was dead, and her life, the other members said, was past, like a blown-out flame and didn't matter because it was gone. But Rachel knew about flames and scars. She held her sleeves in her hands, and thought about Benny's life and what it was like, even though she knew she was breaking the rules, and that if she remembered one thing she might begin to remember others too.

When the woman came later to light the fire, and the ceremony began, she looked at Rachel for a long time, as she stood in the circle. It was like she was thinking about the night before, Rachel thought, which didn't exist anymore, just like Benny didn't. They couldn't talk about it when the other members were around. Rachel was thinking, too, about Benny, and how the woman's bread-hands had touched her. The woman, who was no longer a member, could think about the past as much as she wanted to. Rachel could see that it worried her, like a page in a book that made no sense. Then Rachel began to feel bits of her memories, which she had forgotten, come creeping back in to the corners of her head, and she decided that it was the woman's hands and thinking about Benny that did it.

After the burning, the woman said that Benny had been reincarnated in a place of peace, had been made into a tree and would live for six hundred years. The members continued as before and forgot the past that had Benny in it.

But while the fire was still lit and the other members were just beginning to go back inside after the hand holding, and the head was too hot to go near, Rachel ran into the library, and sat at the desk again, as she had earlier, reading anything to keep the story of the past coming back in with the knife and candles and cigarettes. She had found the story of Odysseus killing the Cyclops in the painted book again. She was reading the page where Odysseus tells the Cyclops that his name is Nobody and the Cyclops shouts 'Nobody is killing me' as he is blinded with a fiery stake. Rachel read and read, not seeing the words, until the woman with the green eyes found her and took her by the arm and led her outside, so that they could talk. It was dark. They moved across the gardens quickly, towards the fire where the remains of Benny's body lay. *Nobody is killing me,* Rachel said to herself, over and over. *Nobody is killing me.* If she stopped, she thought of the knife-feeling in her stomach, which had her old memories in it.

The woman took her over to a tree near the herb garden, and she could smell the sage and the night air. The flames were lower now than before, but they still burnt strongly.

'One of the stones last night said death, and I was frightened,' the woman told Rachel. Frightened of the stones, Rachel thought, now she knew what frightened the woman – the stones that she carried with her all the time.

The woman put her hand under Rachel's hood and touched her face, then she put her hands on her waist under her top, and they kissed each other slowly. After that evening, whenever she kissed anyone, Rachel remembered smoke and sage.

'What were the other stones?' Rachel asked.

'Sit down and I'll show you.' They sat down on the grass, which was damp, and the woman took out her stones again, and handed the three that had frightened her to Rachel.

'This is death.' It was the yellow stone with the cross. 'Because it was this way up.' The woman turned it over. 'And at the top of the triangle. This one is ink, and this one is memories. Together they mean fire.'

'Benny's fire?'

'Yes.'

'Memories aren't allowed.'

'I know. It frightened me. Death, memories and fire

together.'

'And ink?'

'Write.'

'Write what?'

'Your memories.'

'I don't have any. We're not allowed. That's the point of being here.'

'I used to be a member. I know what the rules are.'

'No before or after.'

'What about Benny?' Rachel didn't answer, instead she thought about the knife in her stomach. When the woman was gone, she thought, she would have to go to the kitchen to find a knife. She would be safe. Everyone was asleep. The woman touched her face again.

'Can I stay with you tonight?' she said.

'You're not allowed,' said Rachel sharply, thinking about the kitchen. 'You're not a member. Strangers who haven't forgotten can't sleep at the House, and sex can only be with other members.' So the woman went back over to the fire, and didn't say anything else.

Rachel went and found a knife. She meant to take it up to her room, where there were so many things that no-one would notice one more, but she couldn't wait, so she went into the library instead where the desk with the word marks was, and sat down. She rolled up her sleeve, and ran the blade over her arm. There was her blood, singing and whispering. But just a few memories trickled out onto her arm, the rest stayed inside. She wanted to get rid of them all, to cut and cut until they were gone. She raised the knife again. But the door to the library opened suddenly. There was no-one there, although Rachel felt cold, as if there were a spirit in the room. Benny's spirit, she thought, and she put down the knife. But then there was the woman with the bread hands in the doorway, looking at the blood on Rachel's arm and on the table and the knife. She didn't say anything at first. She went and got damp tissues from the bathroom and mopped up the blood. The cuts weren't deep and they stopped bleeding quickly. Then she went and got some of the thin sheets of paper that Rachel used for writing her letters, and a blue pen, and put them on the desk.

'Go on,' she said. That night, the woman watched while Rachel wrote down her memories, which had flooded back into her stomach when she saw Benny on the fire, and when the woman touched her arms. The woman sat next to her and watched, while Rachel wrote page after page in blue ink. She wrote quickly, as if she couldn't stop, but when she did, the woman undressed and told Rachel to do the same, like it was a normal thing to undress in the library with the books watching. Rachel sat on the woman's lap, and they kissed again in different places, and twisted around each other, until they were on the floor next to the desk, turning over and over, with the memories on the paper above them. Rachel could smell smoke and sage.

In the morning, one of the members found Rachel's memories, remembered and on the desk in the library. But Rachel and the woman with green eyes had gone through the white gate and along the winding paths towards the sea, and they were past and gone like leaves. The spaces that they left closed behind them, and the members of the House forgot about them, and did not remember.

Red Roof

My hats are made from wool. Some are brown and orange, but most of them are green or grey. Once, years ago, when I was sixteen and hadn't been on the markets long, I sold hats at an outside market stall in November and it was very cold. The woman at the stall next to mine told me she was a farmer. Her smile was so big it took up half her face. She already had a hat and it nearly covered her eyes. She looked cold and thin, but she smiled at everyone until her top gum showed. She had a thick coat on and she talked to every customer: the woman with the jumper with small stripes and big glasses, the grey man with the hat and green coat, the small child with mittens and something yellow and sticky round its mouth.

I sold hats. The woman with the big smile sold everything: slabs of cake, pots of feta, honey, plum pickle. The turnips were purple and the size of children's heads and when I curved my hand around one of them it was rough and solid. There was thick green spinach and rough carrots and parsnips curling into shapes, like they had only just come out of the ground. I didn't have a tablecloth, but hers was yellow with printed roses.

She had a black dog with one ear and a grey nose; it limped around her table on three good legs. The smell of the sea was in the air and I could smell it on her too. It was like her scent. She wore it along with her smile. Maybe it hung around her like a cloud. We were next to each other all day, and she soon worked out that I was young, and I minded her stall while she went for tea and sugar for both of us, then she told me about some of the places I had never heard of. She told me about Red Roof, and said she was going to go one day again and I could come too, so it was because of the woman who smiled with her teeth and her gums that I went to Red Roof for the first time.

'Red Roof is an indoor market,' she told me, sipping her tea. I couldn't see her eyes properly; because of the way they were hidden by her hat.

'Upstairs,' she said, 'there is a room called the Top Room, and if you pay you can have a space to sleep for the night and a pillow; though you need your own sleeping bag, and you get warm bread and coffee when you wake up, or honey and water. Usually the Top Room is for people who have come a long way to the market, who don't want to travel there and back again. People who want to stay to sell their things all weekend.'

The first time I went to Red Roof, it was with the smiling woman and her dog. We closed the big black door behind us and stood for a while, looking. From the doorway, I could see how big the market was. It was so big and there were so many people that I could hardly see where it ended, though I made out some stairs on the far side. We went in, and my companion with the big smile, who was still wearing her hat, began to set up her stall. I didn't have my own table. A woman with a red jumper, who was in charge, told me to follow her, and we pushed our way through the crowd. She showed me to a spare table in a corner, a long way from the only person in the room I knew, who waved at me and went on arranging her cabbages. On the way, I saw snatches of the other market stalls between the people, some with food, others with glass jars or clothes. The hall was big and dark and people moved around drinking cups of hot wine and spices and eating chocolate bread or gingerbread cake. I saw a girl with messed up blonde hair and fish blue eyes a few steps away from me as we went through the hall. She turned to look, but the woman in the red jumper was moving quickly and soon we were gone into the crowd of people.

I laid out my hats. On the stall next to mine there were butternut squashes and slabs of cheese - some of it was green with herbs - and bags of garlic and white pots of olives and under the table there were big sacks of potatoes. After a while, I left my stall in the hands of the man who owned the cheese and vegetables and went to look round. It was a witch's cauldron place, full of smells and spells and people. Light was flickering, mainly from the fire and candles. A thick purple curtain hung over a door at the back behind the stairs. The floor was made of grey stone and there was a log fire in the middle of the wall next to my table, with big arm chairs around it. While I had set up my stall, two children bounced up and down on the chairs and stood on their heads. They were small, both girls, about two and a half feet tall, one with brown hair to her shoulders, and the other with a dark brown afro twisted into tight curls. And I saw one woman dancing by herself in the corner. Soft music played behind her, which I heard when I went nearer. It had a fast beat, but most people didn't hear it, so she looked like a goddess twisting to herself, with six arms and seven eyes - an eye in each hand and one on her forehead. She had black hair.

There was a counter in the corner by the door where we had come in where two women with tight white aprons and ginger hair - maybe they were sisters, I thought - served people. I went over to look. There were spicy drinks - mango and cinnamon, ginger and carrot, apple, ginger and honey - frothed up together in a mixer behind the counter.

One of the sisters smiled over at the man behind a table nearby. He was selling instruments. He wore a red hat because away from the fire it was cold, and the flaps at the side came down over his ears. There were big pipes and drums with skins stretched over them. Lots of people stood around his table, so I couldn't see very well. He juggled with red and yellow juggling balls, and people tried out the drums and the stringed instrument he had put at the front of the table. I wandered back to my stall and looked over to the other side of the room to where my companion with the big smile had forgotten me. She was selling a round turnip to an old man with a stick. The dog with one ear was sitting with its head on its paws in front of the table.

When I looked back, there was the girl with blue eyes I had seen before. She was playing with my hats. She had hair like sand or hair like you get when you stand on the beach with your face in the wind for so long that the salt gets mixed in with your hair and messes it up. She had blue eyes like blue fish or like the flames at the heart of the fire if you watch it and watch it until there's nothing else in your head apart from the fire and your face is hot from watching, then you might see a little blue flame under one of the burning logs and feel like Shedrach in the fire. She had eyes that were that kind of blue. She was wearing a green jumper with a white star on the front and dark blue jeans. She didn't buy a hat. I noticed when I was close to her for a second time that she was about the same age as me. She saw me looking at her and moved on to another stall. When I had finished serving a customer, she was picking up silver earrings from a different table and holding them up so she could see them and twisting them round so they caught the light. She didn't buy any earrings either. I watched her push her way through the crowd and towards the stairs. She went up quickly. I didn't see her come back down again and I thought she must have stayed in the Top Room that the smiling woman had told me about.

Even though it was still daylight outside it felt like evening inside. Once you were inside, you couldn't tell whether it was day or night. Once you were inside, you couldn't see the stone walls or the patterns on the outsides of the windows. Now I have been back to Red Roof a hundred times I know that there are shutters on the inside so you can't see out, but my first time, when I was sixteen, I just knew it felt dark and smoky. Also, I know now that you can only see the red roof from outside, and that outside the walls are painted green and big iron letters hang on one wall. They spell out the name of the hall: *Red Roof*.

Now I've been back again and again, I know that the hall is called Red Roof because the roof is made of red stone and it's flat, so that if you climb up the stairs away from the hall where the people are and into the Top Room, and if you stand on a chair and push yourself up and out of the skylight, the one next to where the chimney stack goes, if you climb up and out of the window you can stand and watch the street below if you want to. If you want to, you can see the people in thick coats hurrying up the street with their hats pulled over their eyes and ears against the cold, with their turnips and potatoes and slabs of cake. You can turn your face up towards the grey sky and watch the white screwed up balls of hail start to fall and crunch up your eyes and nose as they fall on your face. Balls of hail that sting like electric shocks and make you feel like you are alive and not dead. Little orgasm things falling on your face so cold you think your face might turn blue or grey like the sky and you think you might turn into part of the cloud and step off the roof and swoop over the other roof tops that aren't red but are grey like the cloud. Standing on top of the red roof you can see a blue grey line where the sea is, but you can't see the orange buoys bobbing on the grey waves, or the adolescent white and brown seagulls spreading their wings and hooking their beaks. Down by the seafront the sleeping masks of the yachts sing like bells in the wind. If you were there, in the winter like it is now, down by the harbour, the wind would be cold on your cheeks and the wind would blow the hail towards you from the sea and you wouldn't be able to look anymore. Or if you walked up the hill a little way from Red Roof, you would get to the top of the hill and then you could see the grey sea spread out like a picnic blanket underneath you. You could watch the night creep in around the rocks and sit still over the water from the top of that hill. You could think about the turnips with purple children's faces and the ice in your hair.

When you go back inside Red Roof, you'll see that some people are leaving. Some people have sat down in the chairs by the fire and have lit tightly rolled cigarettes or brown pipes that smell sweetly of herbs, and are drinking chamomile and honey out of big mugs. Now people are leaving, if you listen carefully; above the fire crackling, you can hear the yachts singing in the distance, and hear the brown and white seagulls crying to themselves in the cold. The dog with one ear lies down by the fire, and before he closes his eyes you can see they are milky-white, and that he's old and tired. He sleeps. You can see he is dreaming when his tail moves. The fire spits and you can smell lavender from a large green pot on the hearth.

My first time, when I was sixteen, I didn't know about the harbour or the skylight or the singing yachts. When the day and most of my hats had gone, and when the hall was beginning to empty of people, I saw that the woman with the big smile who had brought me was packing up her table and her turnips. I could smell the fire and cinnamon and lavender that was left over as the people went. I looked over to the stairs. I remember thinking that the girl with the messed up hair and fish-blue eyes hadn't come back down from the Top Room. I remember a feeling like I wanted to be in the same room as her. The emptying hall felt uncomfortable without her there. I knew that the Top Room was serious, because the woman with the big smile had been there before to play, and I remember wondering what they were playing that day. I wondered what her name was, and whether I could get to talk to her if I played too, and I hoped I knew the game they were playing.

So when there were no more customers, I wrapped my remaining hats in the blanket I had brought to sleep on. Then I got hot apple and cinnamon from the counter and went up stairs to the Top Room, where there was pink carpet on the floor, and where a group of people had gathered around a table and weren't smiling. The girl with the sandy hair was there but she didn't look up. They were all concentrating. Only the woman in the red jumper who had shown me my table looked up when I came up the stairs. She had brown hair in a ponytail and lines around her mouth and her eyes, which made her look dangerous, like she knew things, but safe and warm at the same time. I sat down at a table nearby with my drink steaming and stashed my hats and blanket under the chair.

I could see from the pictures on the cards that they were playing Scrummage. I felt pleased because I knew how to play, because my father had taught me the cards before I could read. I wanted to join in, but I didn't say anything. I watched first because I wanted to be invited. I watched the next round. I saw who had the Ghost Card from where I was sitting, and who had the Brown Girl but I didn't move or show it on my face. I knew better. I looked around the Top Room. Over in the corner a curtain had been hooked against the wall and I saw that behind it there were three mattresses piled one on top of the other and some thick blankets with two or three big pillows. Looking at the makeshift bed made me wonder who would get to sleep on it. It looked much more comfortable that the rugs and mattresses and cushions thrown around the rest of the room. Then someone on the other side of the table, the man sitting next to the woman I wanted to talk to, played the Red Jester and the spell was broken, and everyone sat back in their chairs and stretched and someone lit a cigarette; someone else ran off downstairs for more tea. People laughed and yawned and gathered up the cards.

'You know it?' the woman with the red jumper asked me.

'Yes,' I said.

'Come and play.' I pulled my chair nearer. 'I'm Ann, by the way.' She made space for me.

'Faith,' I said. Some of the others nodded. The girl with sandy hair looked up at me but didn't nod or say anything. No one introduced me to anyone else. They were used to knowing each other and used each other's names easily. I learnt a few straight away:

'Sit down, Patty,' the man next to me said to a big woman wearing dungarees. Patty smiled at him and sat down beside him. She had braided hair and the beads caught the light as she moved her head around.

'Simon's turn to deal,' said Ann. Simon was the man who had won the last game. It seemed as though Ann was in charge of games as well as tables. We picked up our cards. Mine weren't good. The Two of Rakes, the Yellow Feather Man and the Prince of Grass. I smoothed the cards with my thumb and wondered how many fingers had touched the pictures. I liked the colours and the way the clothes had been drawn. I imagined someone making a picture of me to put on a card. If someone did, would I be caught there on the card like a red leaf that looks like a caught butterfly in the road, or like a man trapped in a mirror?

'Your turn,' said Ann. I could feel everyone's eyes on me.

'What's her name?' I heard someone say.

'My name's Faith,' I said.

'Faith,' someone whispered.

'Scream,' I said, quietly: I had wanted to make a good impression, but now I felt very shy. I put down the Two of Rakes and picked up a card from the pile. The Knife Card. It was a red card, and it might have been useful if I'd had anything higher. It wasn't a promising start. I could see the more experienced players noting behind their eyes that I didn't have good cards. I took a sip of my drink.

'Grab,' said the man next to me and put down the Nab of Sixes. He took three more cards from the pile. Now no one was smiling. Everyone was back into the game as if they had never left it, apart from a slight feeling of difference because Ann had admitted me, an extra player.

Patty looked at her friend quickly and laid down the Man of Mirrors. It was a yellow card. The edges gleamed under the light like they were made of gold. Further round the circle someone had the Boy of Mirrors and won the hand. Everyone breathed out together. One man, who had a beard, lit a pipe. The next round began.

The girl with messy hair who's name I didn't know yet said, 'Scream.' She put down the Red Hen and picked up another card. Our discarded cards, the Two of Rakes and the Red Hen, sat side by side in the scream pile. She flashed a look at me. We were the only two screamers so far. I held onto the look she'd given me inside my head. It was good to feel her looking at me with her blue fish eyes.

Ann reached over and touched the girl's hand like she'd known her for ten years and loved her easily.

'The Red Hen,' Ann said, and stroked the back of her hand, 'not so good this time, Star.' I wondered if Star was her real name or if it was a nickname. It looked from Ann's score sheet as if Star had held a lot of high risk cards early on, but had won some good hands. It looked like the game might be between Simon and her, but it was hard to tell, reading Ann's writing upside down. Then Simon smiled to himself and played the Green Jackdaw, and everyone sighed and handed over their highest green cards. Reluctantly, I gave up the Prince of Grass. Though the card was worthless, I liked the picture of the man in the green feathered hat with a pink sweet pea in his hand and shiny eyes.

The Jackdaw is supposed to be a chance to see what high cards other people have been holding onto. I knew I wouldn't win now, so I didn't take in the cards that other people passed over, although I looked at Star's card. The Green Spider. Quite good, I thought, a hard one to give up. I wondered if I could call her Star, or if I had to wait until I could touch the back of her hand like Ann had done. Simon collected up his new cards and looked around the table slyly.

'Be careful, Simon,' said Patty. If someone played the Red Jester or the Ghost Card now Simon would lose a lot of points, but when it came to Patty's turn she was a screamer too. She put the Blue Hen next to the red one.

'What are we playing for?' I whispered to Ann suddenly. I had forgotten to ask, and now I wasn't going to win I felt like I could without sounding ambitious. I hoped it wasn't too serious. When I was that age, I didn't play the serious games when I came across them and I was usually careful to ask first, or look at people's faces to see. This time I hadn't been so careful because I wanted to be in the same room as the girl with the messy hair. Ann motioned to the next player to put down a card.

'The bed,' said Ann simply. I looked over to the corner again, to where the three mattresses were piled behind the curtain. No wonder people had looked at me uneasily when I had started to play, though even if I had won all the remaining hands, it would have been hard for me to get anywhere on the score sheet because I'd come in halfway through.

Then it was Star's turn again. She had the Red Jackdaw. She must have picked it up last time round, I thought.

'That's better,' said Ann, and smiled at her. If anyone had the Red Jester they would have to hand it over. The players all waited as one by one we put down our cards. The man with the beard had it. He must have been waiting till his hand was stronger. People gasped when he had to hand it over. It was risky to play the Red Jackdaw. Now everyone knew Star could win on her next go if she wanted to. If her hand was strong enough. Anyone with the Ghost Card was likely to play it. We looked at each other. People played their strongest cards.

When I put down the Knife, people pulled faces and said, 'Faith, you had it all along,' and I felt like I was part of the game. No one had the Ghost. When it was Star's turn again, Simon said, 'Go on, Star,' good-naturedly. She smiled, and it was the first time I'd seen her smile. I noticed that she had a tiny piece of crystal fixed to one of her teeth, like an earring in her mouth. Maybe that's why she's called Star, I thought. She played the Red Jester.

'Time,' said Ann, looking at her watch.

'One more?' said Simon.

'We agreed the time,' said Ann. Everyone nodded. Ann spent a moment leaning over her score sheet, but it seemed as though people already knew the outcome. The man with the beard had gone off down the stairs for another drink, and a couple of people had started chatting and shuffling their cards absentmindedly.

'Star wins on points,' said Ann. People started to move away from the table. Some went to claim a sleeping space, and some broke open big bars of chocolate. I stayed where I was at the table. Ann gathered the cards together, took the band out of her hair and wrapped it around the cards, so that her hair fell over her shoulders, then she got up and left us too. She squeezed Star's shoulder as she went past and down the stairs. The next time I saw Ann, she was sitting by the fire with a silver pipe in her hand, listening to the man with the beard tell stories.

It was just Star and me at the table. She smiled again, and I saw her fish eyes and the star on her tooth. I wondered how to talk to her. It would be nice, I thought, to trace the shape of her face with my finger and put my fingers in her mouth. It would be nice, I thought, to be able to see whether she was thinking about the game or the prize or me.

'I'm going to get some food,' I said, because I couldn't think of anything else, 'do you want some?' She shrugged.

'Maybe later,' she said. Not about me then, I thought, and I got up and made my way back downstairs. It was getting late, and most of the people who weren't staying had gone home. I walked all the way across the hall, around the few lingerers, and the sellers packing up their things, to the counter in the corner. There was only one ginger-haired sister serving now. I ordered fried potato and cheese and sat down on a stool to wait.

'And apple, cinnamon and ginger,' I said, and put down my money. She poured me a glass, and I let the steam warm up my face and the hot glass warm up my hands. I looked around the hall. The woman with the big-gummed smile had folded up her table completely and was sitting on a chair with her black dog at her feet. Although we had come together, I still didn't know her name. She was talking to the man who sold the instruments. He had packed all his unusual objects away and there was no sign of them. On the side of the hall near where the stairs where, I could see the woman who had been dancing earlier, dancing again, with another woman this time. They looked like Gemini twins dancing together. My father showed me a picture of the signs of the zodiac once, where the Gemini twins carried water pots on their heads. I imagined the dancing women with pots on their heads, using one hand to steady them and seeing some of the water splashing over the edges and onto the floor. Over by the wall, on the far side of the hall, more people sat eating corn and soup. Then I looked over to the fire, and saw that Star had come downstairs and was sitting with Ann, eating raspberries from a bowl. She must have changed her mind about food, I thought, and I felt jealous of the fire. I was cold over in the corner, but I was too shy to go and sit with them without the cards to hide behind.

She must have seen me looking, because just as the ginger haired sister put my potato and cheese down in front of me with a fork, Star got up and made her way towards me, around the sacks of potatoes that still stood in the middle of the hall and the tiny sculptures of round people with big eyes and some blue bottles, which someone was packing away carefully into a case. She sat next to me. There was a trace of raspberry juice around her mouth. She ordered hot wine, but wouldn't let me pay for it.

'You were looking at me,' she said.

'I was thinking about the fire,' I said, half telling the truth.

'Are you cold?' she said.

'A bit.'

'You've got nice hands,' she said, looking at the way I held my glass. My cheeks felt hot when she said that. I looked down at my hands.

'Thanks,' I said. She smiled. 'You have to say something back now.'

'Sorry.' I wanted to say you've got beautiful eyes and your hair looks salty and I like that thing you've got in your mouth, but I didn't. Instead I said: 'You're good at Scrummage.'

'Have you got a coat?' she said.

'Yes,' I said. I had a big grey fleece, which I had hung up in the corner, near where my hat table had been.

'It's cold outside, but I want to show you.'

'Show me what?' I said. She didn't answer.

'Finish that,' she said and pointed to my dinner, 'and meet me outside.'

'Why?'

'I like you,' she said and pulled my earlobe slowly like she knew me already.

Outside, the stars shone through holes in the deep grey clouds, and I saw the full moon once before it disappeared. We went down the hill and turned the corner, and there was the sea in front of us, and the yachts and the smell of sand and crabs. We went and stood right on the edge of the harbour, with our toes over the edge, and looked at the boats and the rocks that curled round to make the bay. I was very cold now. Star had been warmed up by the fire before she came out, and still had a bit of the fire inside her. She picked up my hands and rubbed them between hers until they were tingling.

'Now put them in your pockets,' she said, and I did.

'What are you going to show me?' I said.

'Wait,' she said. Then she led me away from the harbour and over to the little stony beach that sat quietly by itself waiting for morning. The stones were covered in black seaweed, because the sea had been rough earlier, though it was a little calmer now. Star looked up at the sky and said, 'More hail tonight, probably.' I nodded, and we went down onto the beach.

'Have you been here before?' she said.

'No,' I said. She walked along the rocks that formed the edge of the beach until she came to a shallow cave that suddenly cut into the black rock.

'Here,' she said, and she sat down inside the cave and motioned for me to sit down next to her. Then she picked up something that was lying next to where she was sitting and handed it to me. It was a skull. Probably a sheep or a goat. The skull had been worn smooth by the sea. I felt it with my hand.

'I think it drowned,' she said, and took it from me again. 'A long time ago.'

'Is that what you wanted to show me?'

'No. Just this,' she said quietly, and pointed out of the cave towards the beach and the sea, which was framed by the cave mouth and was grey-black and fringed with white fists, which were pummelling the stones like they were angry. The dark clouds hung over the sea like giant parachutes.

'It's beautiful,' I said, though my words were taken away by the night as soon as I had said them. They sounded too loud, and next time I spoke, I spoke quietly, like she had done.

'And I want to kiss you,' she said, so quietly I could hardly hear her at all, 'but I didn't want to do it in there with everyone watching.'

'I thought you didn't want to talk to me after we played upstairs,' I said.

'I'm just shy.'

'Me too.' We didn't do anything. We sat looking out at the sea bashing the stones with its fists, like the beach was a door and the sea was demanding to be let in. I turned round and saw her eyes flashing at me like fish again. I kissed her with the sound of the sea getting angrier in front of us. She was as soft as sand. When we looked up again the hail had started. We linked arms and ran back to Red Roof with the hail stinging our necks and ears, and our faces tucked as far inside our coats as they would go. When we got back most people had gone to bed. There was no one by the fire, so we sat and got warm again.

'Is Star your real name?' I asked. She didn't say anything. Instead she rolled up her sleeve and showed me her left arm. There was a scar from her wrist up to her elbow in one long line. I ran my finger along it. The line was softer than the skin around it and pinker.

'I fell on a broken window when I was small,' she said, 'then it was my nickname. My parents called me Scar and when I went to school, the other kids called me it too.'

'That's nasty,' I said. I ran my finger over the scar again. It was beautiful, I thought, but I didn't say it.

'Ann's my foster Mum,' she said. 'She's in charge of Red Roof. She said I should get a star in my mouth and tell everyone that my name is Star not Scar. So I did.' We kissed again for so long that the side of my face nearest the fire got really hot. I put my hand up to feel her face and she was hot too.

'I'm tired,' she said, and stood up. 'I want to go to bed.' I thought for a second she was going to sleep on the three mattresses without me, but then she said, 'Come on,' and pulled me up too. We climbed up the stairs together and stepped over the sleeping bodies quietly. Ann was curled up asleep in the corner on one of the small mattresses. We got onto the bed and pulled the curtain around us. I pulled the blankets into shape. We both took our trousers off quickly because it was cold, and got underneath. We could hardly see each other now the curtain was closed. She picked up my left hand and kissed it.

'You've got nice hands,' she said.

'You told me,' I said.

'You have to say something back now.'

'OK, you've got nice eyes and hair, and I like your shiny tooth thing and your scar.'

'You used them all up at once,' she said. I put my hands on her waist and said that no those weren't the only things. I took my top off, then I helped her lift off hers and I kissed her again, and it felt like we were the same person for a long time until I opened my eyes and heard drumming on the roof and skylight, and I thought it might be the angry sea wanting to get in. She put her head on my chest and I could feel her hair on my neck and smell how salty it was. It wasn't the sea. It was the hail knocking on the roof, banging so hard, and the wind, blowing so strongly that we couldn't sleep and we both lay awake in the dark with our eyes open, listening.

The Grandma Tree

My grandmother liked knitting, and she made me wind her wool up for her in tight balls. Before the kitten drowned, it liked to chase my grandmother's wool across the floor. Sometimes different colours, green, blue, pink, purple, would criss-cross each other from the kitten-wool game if my sister had been playing for a long time. It depended what my grandmother was making. If she made something multi-coloured, and my sister played for a long time, then it would happen. Once, my grandmother made me a stripy scarf that went all the way down to the floor. Another time, she made me a jumper to go with the scarf. When she was doing that, the wool went to and fro across the floor in a giant Technicolor spider's web. I wound it up carefully afterwards. I didn't mind doing it. I liked it. The fire jumped around excitedly. My grandmother's needles went click click click. My sister held the kitten to the window so she could watch the snow falling. I could smell dinner simmering in the kitchen. I wound the wool back up tight into balls and arranged them in her knitting bag, like jumper seeds ready to spring into life.

My grandmother would sit in the kitchen with me sometimes while I drank milk and took bites out of my sandwich so they made a pretty pattern. She put her arm around me and said she was going to tell me a story. Her stories would always start in the place where we were. If we were in the garden, under the oak tree, that's where it would start. Once, there were two birds sitting in an oak tree. If we were by the pond, that's where it would start. Once, there were seven sisters who sat and sewed by a shining silver pond. If we happened to be strolling through the garden and kicking the leaves with our feet, it would begin there. Once, two boys shuffled through the leaves and ate baked potatoes as they walked. Or: Once, there were seven sisters who stood in the autumn wind and played with each other's hair. Sometimes it started in the kitchen.

'I knew a woman who told me about a girl who liked to sit at her kitchen table all day long,' my grandmother said. She put her arm around me when she told her stories. Her arm told the story as well. If it got frightening, she would hold me tighter. If there was a storm on a boat, she would rock me to and fro. If there was a wishing well, she would move her hand to my shoulder, and we would pretend to look into the well together to make our wish and wait to see if it came true. If two people fell in love, she would stroke my elbow and gaze into the distance as if she was remembering the time she fell in love with my grandfather. That was in a field. I knew because she had told me about lying on her back in the grass. Her arm was like a thick rope binding me to the tale.

I had a crush on the gardener's daughter. She had blonde hair and a turned up nose and she sat cross-legged under the window, next to the dog roses. I leant against the oak tree, sewing beads onto my purse and watched her. I liked her blue eyes. They shone whenever she looked at me. She gave me an earthy feeling, or rather, a turned up earth feeling, like someone was digging there, turning me over. I sat down next to her and crossed my legs too. She looked at me solemnly and didn't say anything at first. She just dug around in the earth with a stick.

'See the oak tree?'

'Yes,' I said.

'I bet I can hang from that branch by my knees, with no hands.'

'OK then,' I said. She checked to make sure her father wasn't looking, ran over to it, climbed quickly, and hung from the strongest branch, upside down, her hair falling towards the ground, her arms dangling, her T-shirt falling over her face. I watched. After a while, she righted herself and ran back over.

'Does it hurt?' I said.

'A bit,' she said and shrugged. After that, we gazed up into the branches together and they criss-crossed over our heads. Then I heard my middle sister coming, and for some reason I didn't want her to know we were there, so I pulled my new friend behind the tree trunk. No-one could see us anyway, the branches hung down towards the earth like a skirt. The gardener's daughter giggled as we watched my middle sister's feet go past. I suddenly felt happy, being next to her and next to the trunk of the oak. All summer, we lay under the branches of the old oak together and looked up and the criss-cross roof above us. One day we were lying on our backs and it was cold. She gave me her jumper and I draped it over both of us, so it was like we were in bed together. I thought it was funny.

'What?' she said.

'Nothing,' I said. I was embarrassed.

'I'm going away,' she said, suddenly. I sat up so I was leaning on my elbows.

'Why?' I said.

'For gardening school. My Dad's sending me.'

'How far away?' I said.

'I don't know. A long way.' She dug in her pocket like she was digging in the earth and pulled out a silver sphere on a long chain. She held my hand and pressed it into my palm.

'What is it?'

'Open it,' she said. I did as she told me. I lifted the lid and watched as a needle bobbed over a curling N for North. A compass.

'To show you the way,' she said.

I cried when she left. It felt, not like a friend leaving, but like I had lost my arm or my tongue or my foot. I had that same phantom sense that the lost thing was still there, haunting me.

My pet guinea pig died on the day she left. My father told me and my six sisters to bury it in the muddy patch beyond the oak tree. I wrapped the small black body in cloth and laid it in the grave. As I watched my eldest sister cover it over, I cried and they thought I was crying for my pet, but I wasn't. I was frightened that a tree would grow up on the spot where we had planted her, a whole tree of guinea pigs, which would start out as giant black and brown flowers and blossom into squeaking furry bundles wrapped in see through silky leaves, waiting to fall like apples. How frightening it would be to stand under the tree and listen to the squeaking. But though I waited, and looked out of the window, at the fallen brown leaves, at the snow and the hard ground, at the new green buds, the guinea pig tree didn't grow. Even though I had been frightened, I watched even harder, for longer, because I thought that maybe watching made it happen.

One night, when it got truly dark, and everyone else was in bed, I crept outside. I knelt down near to, but not quite next to, where my pet guinea pig lay, put my hands into the dark earth and let it crumble between my fingers. Then I dug a bit deeper. I scooped out a whole handful and then another and another until I had a hole. Quickly, I dipped my hand into my pocket and pulled out the purse I had made myself out of soft pink cloth and coloured beads. The beads made a spiral pattern like a wave across the surface in blue and white. I watched the wave for a while, but I didn't press my fingers to it like I wanted to because they were caked in earth from digging. I held the purse carefully trying not to get it muddy. All the same, when I opened the clasp, I left two fingerprints either side like I had committed a crime. I took out the silver compass the gardener's daughter gave me from inside and settled it in the hole I had made. Then I covered it with the soil I had disturbed.

One day in spring, my eldest sister found me behind a curtain and asked me why I was hiding. I couldn't tell her about the guinea pig tree or the compass tree that I might find growing one day below my window with black flowers blowing in the wind, or humming silver berries. I let her sit in the window seat and hold onto me, and I cried into her shoulder. After that, I didn't watch anymore. I felt as if I had changed, like some girls change from playing with dolls to suddenly throwing their dolls down the stairs. I had changed from a girl who watches for a guinea pig or a compass tree to someone else, a new person, as if I had been buried in the earth myself, and now I was shooting up through the soil, pushing up my green fingers, reaching up so my chin and mouth and nose broke the surface, taking a breath, admiring my own trunk. I couldn't have spoken about it then, but I knew it inside, like a tree must know that it's a tree inside its trunk, because it doesn't have a head to think with. I never told anyone about it. It sunk deep into the bit of me that would have been my trunk if I had been a tree myself.

I got a sharp guilty kick in the stomach, from the inside, the first time my sister suggested that we plant a tree, like I was remembering a guilty secret. Like the time when I ate three shortcake biscuits under the covers in the middle of the night. It was like that, when I remembered planting my pet guinea pig and the compass. I was a bit older and taller. My eldest sister had a baby by then. I was an auntie and a godmother.

'Why don't we plant a tree?' she said. 'So the baby can watch it grow.' I wondered how she knew about planting trees, because I hadn't told anyone at all. I hadn't even whispered it into my pillow at night.

My middle sister had a kitten that drowned in the pond. She said that the kitten's ghost slept on her pillow, but I said she was stupid because ghosts don't have to sleep. The kitten that drowned sunk under the water, right down to where the weeds are. We saw its nose and its eyes and then its ears go under. We waited to see if it would fight its way back to the surface, but it didn't; it sunk like a stone. I wondered if my sister watched the pond to see if kitten water lilies would spread across the surface, just like I watched for the guinea pig tree and the compass tree, but I didn't think about it much at all, because it was her kitten and so they would be her water lilies. Anyway. We didn't plant the kitten. It sunk all by itself. I wasn't sure if things grew if you hadn't planted them.

Just after the kitten drowned in the pond, that spring, when the waters were swollen, my grandmother died on the sofa with her knitting needles in her hands. My father decided that she would be buried in the gardens. My sister came to stay with her baby so that she could organise it. She called the priest and the gravediggers and the stonemasons, and ordered wandering flowers around the edges of the stone and *much loved mother and grandmother* for the words. That was when my sister suggested the tree again. That evening we were sitting on the sofa where my grandmother had died. My sister held up an acorn she had found in the garden, under the oak tree, which my father said was four hundred years old.

'Do you know what this is?' she said. She showed it to the baby as well as me, so I wasn't sure who she was talking to at first. Of course I knew what it was.

'It's an acorn,' I said. My sister jigged the baby on her hip. I looked at its bald head and tiny fingers, and remembered that I was a fairy godmother and one day I would have to turn pumpkins into coaches. I wondered how I was going to manage it.

'If you look really really carefully, you can see the oak tree curled up inside it, waiting to come out.' I took it in my hand and looked. I couldn't see the tree at all, but I nodded anyway.

'I can see it,' I said.

'When we have the priest come to put Grandma to sleep in the earth, shall we put the acorn in too?' my sister said. 'Then she can grow into a big tree. As big as the old tree at the bottom of the garden that you can hide under.' I looked at her sharply. I got the inside kick in my stomach. I imagined watching a tree grow from my bedroom window. In the spring, big white flowers would grow, with multi-coloured balls of wool for berries around them. Then in the summer, the flowers would turn into Grandmas, wrapped in cotton, ready to fall.

'A Grandma tree?' I said. My sister smiled, took the acorn back, and put it in her pocket.

'Yes,' she said.

Nothing happened all summer. Through the autumn, the grave with the grey stone was covered in brown leaves. In the winter, it turned white as Grandma's hair. In March, I saw something from my bedroom window. I ran down into the garden before anyone else was up. The Grandma tree had started to grow. I watched it all year long. I sat next to it when the first leaves were unfolding like tiny hands. I felt the thin trunk, which was thinner than my little finger. I phoned my sister. The baby was starting to walk now. I could hear her crying in the background.

'The Grandma tree has leaves now,' I said.

'Good. I'll come over and see it later. Have the others seen it?'

'No,' I said.

'Good. It can be our secret for now, until they find it for themselves.' It was our secret until, one by one, my sisters found the new tree. I watched them from my bedroom window. They went one at a time, when they remembered that Grandma wasn't on the sofa anymore, to look at the stone. It was still cold and their breath sung around their heads as they looked. Two, three, four, five, six. Two knelt to pray. She was religious, but she didn't mind who she prayed to. She prayed to fairies and clouds and trees. Three with a candle, which the wind kissed out. Four with a ball of wool, which she wound around her hand like a rosary. It was the one she kept under her pillow for the dead kitten to play with. Five with a storybook, which she read from early in the morning, and six, who ran back for a watering can. We never visited the tree at the same time. We had our unspoken days. Monday, Tuesday, Wednesday, Thursday, Friday. My eldest sister, who had her baby on her hip, and I were one and seven. Sometimes on a Saturday we stood together, reading the words on the stone, and watching the Grandma tree grow. Sometimes on Sundays, I went on my own.

One Sunday night when the world was quiet, I stood watching the Grandma tree from my bedroom window. I imagined Grandma below pushing up through the soil, reaching up an arm, pushing with her head, straining her fingers, wriggling until she could feel herself being sucked up into the roots and pushing up into the thick trunk. But it wasn't ready for her yet. So Grandma was waiting, I thought, just under the soil, until the trunk and the branches got thick enough to hold her, then she would climb up and sit inside. Then she would push an arm into each branch. She would grow extra arms so she could feel a bit of her inside each one. She would grow extra fingers so she would be in every leaf. But that wouldn't be for a very long time, a hundred years maybe, I thought to myself, until the trunk was thick enough. Just then I noticed, glinting in the moonlight, a bush had grown up around the Grandma tree for a skirt. It had silver-white branches like fingers of ice. I ran downstairs, and out into the garden. I knelt in front of the silver bush. At the end of each branch were tiny seedpods. I pressed one of them between my thumb and finger, and out fell a silver sphere, tiny, pea-shaped, with a hinged lid. I opened it. I listened carefully. I could hear my guinea pig squeaking like a ghost when I lifted it to my ear.

When I looked over my shoulder, the gardener's daughter was waiting for me in the middle of the frosty grass. She was grown up, but her hair was still in a bob and her nose was still turned up at the edges.

'Hello,' she said. She looked at me with shiny blue eyes.

'My grandma died and now she's growing into a tree,' I said. The gardener's daughter thought about it.

'That's good,' she said. I stood up and took her hand.

Missed Connections

I thought that if I climbed a tree it would be easier. I had put on a bit of weight. I'm not used to climbing trees, but I heaved myself up on to the first branch, over the broken fence. After that I climbed a bit further and held onto the trunk. Illogically, I was afraid of falling. I thought about the fizz and the crackle, but I tried to put it out of my head. I didn't know how the hell I was going to get out of the tree if I changed my mind. I imagined the embarrassment. The firemen with the ladder, my wife's face, how she wouldn't look at me but only past me. There were the train tracks. I knew what time the train was supposed to get here. Bloody trains, always late, even when you were going to throw yourself in front of one. I saw it in the distance, like a giant caterpillar curving round the track towards me. It looked like it was smiling. I saw the driver. It was a woman with bright blonde hair. I wasn't expecting a woman. I looked her in the face for a fraction of a second before I jumped. A jolt, a bang, the sensation of being inside white noise and a washing machine. Pain, like I was being burnt alive from the inside. Longing, for a fraction of a second, to hang on to life for as long as possible; beautiful, fragile life. Then nothing.

❦

I ran across the stone-flagged kitchen in my nightshirt, wishing I had put my socks on. I reckoned I had five minutes. I made tea with the self-consciousness you get from opening someone else's cupboards, even though I was rushing. I had left Bradley asleep, hoping to sneak out, but I needed tea. I have to have tea before I'm properly awake. All Bradley wanted to do last night was talk. How did I feel about it? Hard to tell. Then I admitted to myself, as I finally found the teabags, that I was annoyed. I had wanted sex. He had wanted to talk about books. While the kettle boiled, I turned the radio on, which is how I knew the trains were cancelled. Some kind of disruption on the line. Bugger, bugger, bugger. Texted my boss. Stared at my phone waiting for the reply. *Don't bother coming in.* Followed by: *Your move to Norwich isn't working out. We need to talk.* I slammed the phone on the table. Now what?

I took a big breath and the world suddenly slowed down. I stood rooted to the spot, feet cold on the floor, taking in my surroundings. As I poured water on my tea, I could hear Bradley singing in the shower upstairs. For the first time, I noticed the garden and the wind rattling around it. The maple tapped on the window, its leaves making patterns out of the September sun. Bradley talked about it last night. Paperbark maple - I tossed the name around inside my head - cinnamon coloured with peeling bark.

I opened cupboard after cupboard before I found the sugar. I figured there was no point getting dressed. Instead of running back upstairs I looked around. To one side of a house was an old iron-worked greenhouse, with vine leaves curling around the inside of the roof. I took my tea into the greenhouse and sat on a bench with faded cushions, Japanese-design. Who knew Bradley was a vintage cushion kind of guy? I liked him more because of it. It smelt of earth. I had just put my feet up on a large plant with a hand of sharp leaves and orange flowers, when Bradley came into the greenhouse wrapped in a towel.

'Giant Mexican Aloe Vera,' he said.

'Right,' I said. 'I think I lost my job.'

It was probably Bradley wearing nothing but a towel, the earthy smell in the greenhouse, the tea and the nightshirt, but we wound up doing it right there on the flagstones in his greenhouse. I don't know for certain that was the moment that the sperm went rushing through my cervix into my uterus and fallopian tube in time to meet the tumbling egg, but it was the only time we did it without a condom that month, and anyway, I want to think it happened on the cold stone floor with the arrow-shaped orange flowers of the Giant Mexican Aloe Vera dancing next to us.

❦

On the platform in Sheringham, with a bunch of people ,waiting for a train, I shifted my weight from foot to foot, trying to stay warm, when the robot voice came on: 'We are sorry to announce that all trains have been cancelled due to a fatality on the line. We have no further information at this time.' Everyone reached for their phones.

'All the trains have broken down,' an old woman shouted. She sounded angry at the world. Her face had caved in, her back was bent. She was like a tortoise. A young woman with tattoos arrived late, pulling a suitcase, her toddler running ahead of her, the only one of us who hadn't heard the announcement: a moment of optimism rippling across the station like a stone thrown into a pond.

The guy next to me stabbed his phone impatiently.

'Some idiot has thrown themselves in front of a train,' he said, pacing up and down. I thought about the moment of the leap, the landing, the thud of flesh, metal and bone, and I didn't want to stay there any longer. I thought how much I would like to see the sea. I wandered down Station Road. I got to a junction and saw the fish and chip shop – *The Trawler* – so I bought some and walked on down to the sea front. Even though it was too windy to be there, I sat on the wide steps and ate fish and chips with a wooden fork, looking out at a small white triangle of a boat in the distance. Why did Sam have to come into everything? His face had to appear in my head, right when I wanted to be on my own. I imagined writing about it in my diary later: The sea is the same colour blue as my ex-husband's eyes.

I got up, because it felt like the right moment to be determined to do something, although I didn't know what. I stood with my toes over the edge of the concrete step, wobbling to and fro, beach huts behind me, trying to get rid of Sam's face, trying make myself dizzy, my eyes unfocused, hypnotised by the sky and the concrete and the sea and the salty potato smell of my chips and the sound of the gulls, crying like they were gargling something disgusting.

At that moment I caught sight of the only occupied deckchair on the beach. Because it was so cold, the only others, mainly with dogs, were walking, huddled against the wind. He stood out because he was the only one who wanted to sit. Me and him. I went down the steps. I noticed the side of his face. Probably older than me. Laughter lines, creases, dark stubble. Dotted with grey like paint splatters. I debated with myself whether it was actual paint or not. He was eating an ice cream. I stood at the edge of the beach, chips in hand, watching him, and soon a circle of seagulls stood around my feet like an audience waiting for me to perform. They cried out in chorus. It was then he turned. He smiled, and his face cracked open like a bird hatching out of an egg.

'They've got you trapped,' he said. I smiled back. I clapped my hands - for a moment it looked like I was clapping him - but after a second it worked, the seagulls scattered. I stood next to his chair awkwardly.

'You've got chips,' he said.

'It's what you do at the seaside,' I said. 'You've got ice cream.'

'Ditto,' he said. He looked round, saw a stray deckchair, got out of his own, revealing gangly legs and arms. It took some effort. He dragged the chair over.

'Sit,' he said, and patted it, in a pastiche of chivalry.

'Fancy a chip?' I said. He smiled again. I smiled back.

❦

I'm waiting for my train after my shift, the one that will take me back to him. Our nest, he calls it, but he won't even give me a key, even when I'm home alone. I pace up and down the platform, my sleeves in my hands. The nurse's uniform is too flimsy against the cold. I pull my cardigan tighter. I'm the only one waiting. This station is in a small village, not the nearest one to work; it's away from the main arteries, and that's the way I like it, but why is there never any bloody information? After fifteen minutes, the orange sign saying my train is 'on time' changes to 'delayed'. No shit Sherlock. My phone has died. There's no one in the ticket office. I feel like I am the only person in the world who doesn't know what's going on, like the whole world is happening somewhere else, and everyone else is there. No sound, aside from traffic in the distance and a couple of magpies chattering, definitely not the usual shaking of tracks that means the train is coming; the judder that I don't miss until I can't hear it. I walk up and down for another fifteen minutes. The orange sign changes to 'cancelled'. Nothing else.

I touch the bruise next to my eye and wince. I covered it with make up, but the staff nurse still gave me a funny look, making me wonder if I did a good enough job. There are a couple of others that I don't need to hide with make up because my uniform covers them, but they're bigger and turning yellow and purple like a sunset. The orange sign changes to 'please check our website for updates'.

I wonder what it would be like simply to not exist anymore, to disappear, if only for a day, so I walk to the village pub. They know me in here by my uniform. This is the cosiest pub for miles, and sometimes the old guys at the hospice want to come in here for a final pint, so I wheel them here from the next village, and the landlord, Bobby, helps me hoist them through the door and over the flagstones. So today it doesn't matter that I don't have any money, Bobby keeps me in drinks - tea, a half a cider, more tea - and I sit by the fire with a book from the stack by the window, and he doesn't ask any questions. Mavis, who works in the kitchen, brings me some chips at lunchtime. She slips them in front of me without asking.

'Bobby said to bring you these,' she said. 'You alright love?' I nod. I don't want to talk. I just want to sit. I decide to head home before it gets dark. I say thank you to Bobby, and tell him I owe him one, but he just carries on cleaning glasses and says nothing. Mavis waves at me from the kitchen. I wave back. I pull my cardigan around me against the weather and head towards the station. It seems impossibly cold now. The kind of stone hard cold you get in January.

Back at the station, the ticket office is still deserted, and there's nobody around. I can feel the twilight settling in around me. The bird chatter gets louder, the sky turns saucepan-coloured, the horizon is fringed with red. Still no trains. I shiver, and I feel a sudden stabbing pain, either the bruise complaining, or someone - an unseen someone - has jabbed me in the side, and because I am hypnotised by the cold, and the dusky sky, I decide that someone *has* jabbed me in the side. Not a spirit exactly, although I do believe in spirits, more like a thing, a force. I am a bit of a sci-fi geek. The force jabbed me and said *move* silently but firmly, and I did what it said. I moved. I walked all the way to the end of the platform, where the night time exit was, and pushed the gate open, and kept walking.

The long straight road ran along next to the track. I kept walking. I felt tired and cold, but the hypnotic feeling grew stronger, and the thing, the force, kept jabbing me in the side. *Keep walking,* it said. So I kept walking, the night falling around me like a cloak that I was pulling along with me. *Don't stop,* the force said. I stumbled. I was tired. He was expecting me home hours ago. What if he came out in the car looking for me? *He won't find you out here,* the force said, *he doesn't know*. And no, I thought, he doesn't know that I walk to the next station to save some money, to get some fresh air, to elongate the journey home and the time between work and seeing him. His efforts to check the train times are continually frustrated because the trains are never ever on time, and he knows it, because he takes a train to work himself, in the other direction.

I've been gone all day, I think, *be reasonable. I can't blame that on the trains.* But I could. I could blame it on the trains. The trains had given me a chance to walk. *What else doesn't he know?* The force said. He doesn't know about the cottage. That was a secret I had managed to keep all to myself, even when my mother died, even when the lawyer called about the deeds. Of course, it was a five mile walk from here, but I didn't care about the cold or the road anymore. I stumbled a few times and wiped my face with the back of my hand, but I kept on walking. It was getting dark down here now, away from the village. The trees were shapes, the fence a long line of shadow, still I had heard no train coming either way. I felt as though I was walking in a cloud. I hoped I could remember the way. Over the next hill, keep following the track, and I was sure to hear the sound of the sea and see the green front door, the rough walls, the small windows, the tiny kitchen inside that my mother always kept stocked with big boxes of tea, the sound of the seagulls calling to each other in the cold sky.

Acknowledgements

Thank you to Maria C. McCarthy and Bob Carling at Cultured Llama. Thank you to Naomi Folb for believing in my dyslexic writing. Thank you to Leone Ross for teaching me how short stories work, to the point of obsession - yes, I got it in the end. Thank you to everyone who put up with me writing on location - I was the one in the corner with a cup of tea and a notebook. Thank you to my wife Sarah: still my princess.

'García Márquez is Dead' and 'The Grandma Tree' previously appeared in *Everything is Spherical,* the second anthology of dyslexic literature, in November 2014. 'The First Time' was first published on the *Litro* website in October 2014. 'You Are Not Special' was published on *Litro* in June 2014, and won the Stoke Newington Festival Flash Fiction Competition. 'The Swim' (now 'Kensington Gardens) appeared on *The View from Here* in June 2013. 'The House' appeared in the *Second Diva Anthology of Short Stories* in 2002 and 'Red Roof' was published in *Pretext 5* in 2002.

Note

The first drafts of many of these stories were written on location, often outside or in a café. Sometimes I wrote where I found myself. For instance, when I ended up spending hours in a café in Redruth, in Cornwall - which turned into Red Roof. I began 'Philosophy for Beginners' in The Waffle House, Norwich in 2003, and wrote the rest on the train. More recently, I wrote in a notebook while I waited for two hours for a train in Hassocks ('Missed Connections'). I like writing flash fiction in pubs in Brighton and Hove. 'The Christmas List' was inspired by the (seemingly) random objects in the Alcampo Lounge, a bar and restaurant on the London Road, and I wrote about missing Clissold Park and Abney Park Cemetery in The Brunswick ('You are Not Special').

Sometimes I deliberately set out on a writing trip with a notebook and pen. On these occasions I gave myself some rules. My rules were that the place had to be free to enter, there had to be somewhere to get out of the rain and get a cup of tea, and there had to be something unusual about it. The first of these deliberate writing trips was to Westminster Abbey's College Garden, where I wrote part of a story now called 'Unusual Places'. I also wrote 'Unusual Places' outside London's Guildhall (near the remains of the Roman Amphitheatre), in the Kensington Garden's Orangery, in the Cotton Room at the British Library, and in the Tate Modern members café. I only deviated from my rules once - when I paid to get into the Garden Museum in Lambeth, where I finished 'The Smallest House in London'. (I wrote the first part of this story in a café near Tyburn Convent, Marble Arch - once the site of the smallest house in London.)

I didn't usually write about the place, rather I was inspired by the place. Occasionally I discovered it was impossible to write in the location (in Seven Sisters tube station, for instance, which inspired 'The Grandma Tree') and once or twice I wrote about the experience of being in the place - for instance, in the park in Islington, where I began the opening story, it was too cold to eat my lunch.

Because I lived in London for a long time, many of the places where I wrote 'in situ' were in the capital. 'The First Time' was inspired by the journey between Kings Cross and Finsbury Park, which I used to make regularly. I wrote 'Fragments Found in a Tunnel' in Greenwich Park, near the Isle of Dogs Tunnel. Years ago - before it was renovated - I wrote 'The Marmalade Factory' outside the Chiswick House Glasshouse, which houses rare camellias.

Other stories had more general inspirations. For instance, 'García Márquez and Me' started with a news story of escaped mink in the New Forest, near my town of origin. I eventually finished it and 'The

Grandma Tree' for the second anthology of dyslexic literature, edited by Naomi Folb, so the final drafts of both were written with dyslexic writing in mind. 'The House' started with a paperweight bought for me by my father in a National Trust shop in Dorset, probably Kingston Lacy, though I don't remember for sure.

The stories represent a writing journey that began in 2002 with 'The House'. 'Falling' is the newest, written in 2017. I still write by going on writing adventures, usually by train. In the autumn I took the train from Brighton to St Bee's in Cumbria and back and started a couple of new stories while I was on the move, and I've since invented a detective who gets around 90s London by bike.

Louise Tondeur, June 2018

Cultured Llama Publishing

Poems | Stories | Curious Things

Cultured Llama was born in a converted stable. This creature of humble birth drank greedily from the creative source of the poets, writers, artists and musicians that visited, and soon the llama fulfilled the destiny of its given name.

Cultured Llama aspires to quality from the first creative thought through to the finished product.

www.culturedllama.co.uk

Also published by Cultured Llama

Poetry

strange fruits by Maria C. McCarthy
Paperback; 72pp; 203×127mm; 978-0-9568921-0-2; July 2011

A Radiance by Bethany W. Pope
Paperback; 72pp; 203×127mm; 978-0-9568921-3-3; June 2012

The Night My Sister Went to Hollywood by Hilda Sheehan
Paperback; 82pp; 203×127mm; 978-0-9568921-8-8; March 2013

Notes from a Bright Field by Rose Cook
Paperback; 104pp; 203×127mm; 978-0-9568921-9-5; July 2013

The Fire in Me Now by Michael Curtis
Paperback; 90pp; 203×127mm; 978-0-9926485-4-1; August 2014

Cold Light of Morning by Julian Colton
Paperback; 90pp; 203×127mm; 978-0-9926485-7-2; March 2015

Zygote Poems by Richard Thomas
Paperback; 66pp; 178×127mm; 978-0-9932119-5-9; July 2015

Les Animots: A Human Bestiary by Gordon Meade, images by Douglas Robertson
Hardback; 166pp; 203×127mm; 70 line illus.; 978-0-9926485-9-6; December 2015

Memorandum: Poems for the Fallen by Vanessa Gebbie
Paperback; 90pp; 203×127mm; 978-0-9932119-4-2; February 2016

The Light Box by Rosie Jackson
Paperback; 108pp; 203×127mm; 978-0-9932119-7-3; March 2016

There Are No Foreign Lands by Mark Holihan
Paperback; 96pp; 203×127mm; 978-0-9932119-8-0; June 2016

After Hours by David Cooke
Paperback; 92pp; 203×127mm; 978-0-9957381-0-2; April 2017

There Are Boats on the Orchard by Maria C. McCarthy
Paperback; 36pp; 210×115mm; SKU: 001; July 2017

Hearth by Rose Cook
Paperback; 120pp; 203×127mm; 978-0-9957381-4-0; September 2017

The Year of the Crab by Gordon Meade
Paperback; 88pp; 203×127mm; 978-0-9957381-3-3; October 2017

Flood by Jessica Mookherjee
Paperback; 94pp; 203×127mm; 978-0-9957381-1-9; March 2018

The Other Guernica: Poems Inspired by Spanish Art by Derek Sellen
Paperback; 98pp; 203×127mm; 978-0-9957381-2-6; June 2018

Short stories

Canterbury Tales on a Cockcrow Morning by Maggie Harris
Paperback; 138pp; 203×127mm; 978-0-9568921-6-4; September 2012

As Long as it Takes by Maria C. McCarthy
Paperback; 168pp; 203×127mm; 978-0-9926485-1-0; February 2014

In Margate by Lunchtime by Maggie Harris
Paperback; 204pp; 203×127mm; 978-0-9926485-3-4; February 2015

The Lost of Syros by Emma Timpany
Paperback; 128pp; 203×127mm; 978-0-9932119-2-8; July 2015

Only the Visible Can Vanish by Anna Maconochie
Paperback; 158pp; 203×127mm; 978-0-9932119-9-7; September 2016

Who Killed Emil Kreisler? by Nigel Jarrett
Paperback; 208pp; 203×127mm; 978-0-9568921-1-9; November 2016

A Short History of Synchronised Breathing and other stories by Vanessa Gebbie
Paperback; 132pp; 203×127mm; 978-0-9568921-2-6; February 2017

In the Wild Wood by Frances Gapper
Paperback; 212pp; 203×127mm; 978-0-9957381-6-4; June 2017

A Witness of Waxwings by Alison Lock
Paperback; 128pp; 203×127mm; 978-0-9957381-5-7; December 2017

Dip Flash by Jonathan Pinnock
Paperback; 154pp; 203×127mm; 978-0-9957381-7-1; March 2018

Curious things

Digging Up Paradise: Potatoes, People and Poetry in the Garden of England by Sarah Salway
Paperback; 164pp; 203×203mm; 76 colour illus.; 978-0-9926485-6-5; June 2014

Punk Rock People Management: A No-Nonsense Guide to Hiring, Inspiring and Firing Staff by Peter Cook
Paperback; 40pp; 210×148mm; 978-0-9932119-0-4; February 2015

Do it Yourself: A History of Music in Medway by Stephen H. Morris
Paperback; 504pp; 229×152mm; 978-0-9926485-2-7; April 2015

The Music of Business: Business Excellence Fused with Music by Peter Cook Paperback; 318pp; 210×148mm; 978-0-9932119-1-1; May 2015

The Hungry Writer by Lynne Rees
Paperback; 246pp; 244×170mm; 57 colour illus.; 978-0-9932119-3-5; September 2015

Solid Mental Grace: Listening to the Music of Yes by Simon Barrow
Paperback; 232pp; 210×148mm; 978-0-9957381-8-8; March 2018

Lightning Source UK Ltd.
Milton Keynes UK
UKHW01f1151010918
328159UK00001B/79/P

9 780995 738195